CL

A RUINED SEASON

A RUINED SEASON

JENNIFER MUELLER

THORNDIKE
CHIVERS

This Large Print edition is published by Thorndike Press, Waterville, Maine, USA and by BBC Audiobooks Ltd, Bath, England.
Thorndike Press, a part of Gale, Cengage Learning.
Copyright © Jennifer Mueller 2009.
The moral right of the author has been asserted.

The text of this Large Print edition is unabridged.
Other aspects of the book may vary from the original edition.
Set in 16 pt. Plantin.
Printed on permanent paper.

LIBRARY OF CONGRESS CATALOGING-IN-PUBLICATION DATA

Mueller, Jennifer.
  A ruined season / by Jennifer Mueller. — Large print ed.
    p. cm. — (Thorndike Press large print gentle romance)
  ISBN-13: 978-1-4104-2326-9 (alk. paper)
  ISBN-10: 1-4104-2326-3 (alk. paper)
    1. Scandals—Fiction. 2. London (England)—Fiction. 3. Large type books. I. Title.
PR6113.U35R85 2010
823'.92—dc22   2009041625

BRITISH LIBRARY CATALOGUING-IN-PUBLICATION DATA AVAILABLE

Published in 2010 in the U.S. by arrangement with Robert Hale Limited.
Published in 2010 in the U.K. by arrangement with Robert Hale Limited.

U.K. Hardcover: 978 1 408 47822 6 (Chivers Large Print)
U.K. Softcover: 978 1 408 47823 3 (Camden Large Print)

Printed in the United States of America
1 2 3 4 5 6 7 14 13 12 11 10

Dedicated to George Vincent and Pam Pellini winners of my Create a Hero contest, and Valerie Bongards as winner of the name a pub contest. Their wonderful entries breathed life into my story. And to Tim Krenz for his extensive knowledge of the Napoleonic Wars shared from memory around the camp-fire.

PROLOGUE

London, 1812

Ashe Gardner, Earl of Graemoor surveyed the oak-panelled ballroom as the young women paraded in their best. The girls had all been presented at Court a few days earlier, which meant the season could truly get under way and Ashe's grandmother could get to work in finding him a bride, and he could also get to work in thwarting her every attempt. It wasn't that he abhorred the idea, just the choices that his grandmother pushed in his direction. Most of his dances for this night would be with the young ladies she had pointed out to him as the best prospects. For a dance, they were fine enough; forever after, they would drive him mad. His wife had died only a year after they were wed and ever since mourning was satisfied, his grandmother had been pushing suitable matches his way. She didn't seem to care that he had no trouble finding women, but of course, they weren't wives; not the same thing at all. So now, he was stuck with seventeen- and eighteen-year-old girls who wanted titled husbands. Keeping the ancestral estate running kept him busy enough, not to mention all the parties that he threw to keep his grandmother entertained since she rarely left the house anymore.

Then he spied a true diamond of the first water. Dark ash-blonde hair and slate-blue eyes completed the best countenance he'd seen in a good long while: ethereal pale skin, a long neck setting off an almost regal bearing, tall — statuesque the best word. Perhaps there was a reason to endure the season. Ashe hardly noticed the person who took up position next to him.

'You've got your eye on someone; I know that look.'

Ashe finally pulled his eyes away. 'Who is that, Darnley?'

'Be more specific.'

Ashe looked over at the vision. Didn't he see her? 'There.' Ashe pointed unobtrusively. 'The blonde one. The only one worth looking at.'

'Ahhh, haven't you heard? That's Miss Sophie Greenwood. Her father is Lord Canmore, impoverished as they come and in only the last few days. Her mother tried to marry her off to half the country before it was found out that her twenty thousand pounds was gone in some business misadventure. I received a visit myself before coming to Town. Maybe if she had a title she would be redeemable, but without a farthing. . . .'

'Pity,' Ashe muttered turning away.

Sophie was close enough to hear him, and her heart died that night. How could it not? The news was unknown to her until that moment. If only the ship had gone down several months later after she had secured a husband with her dowry, she wouldn't have to endure her mother's tirades as if it was her fault her father had withdrawn the family money from the bank. He had gambled it, not on a gaming table but on a ship, a ship that should have arrived in a far off port to buy goods worth a fortune even greater. Business, as many would tell her, did not befit people in their position, but with the money that was to be made, her father was willing to risk it. Instead, a hurricane sank the ship and with it her uncle and the fortune her father had entrusted to him, her portion among it. She hadn't known it had been taken out of the bank as well when she had left home. The news had reached the gossips before it reached her own ears. She had watched them, heads together at Almack's, seeking the knowledge that would dash her hopes of a husband. A poor man wouldn't marry her for he would have nothing to support them with. And now she was beneath the touch of a rich man for the shame of allying with a mother who had so splendidly tried to marry her off before news of their financial ruin had reached their ears. Rowengate Park and the barony would pass to her brother Jasper. She was a poor relation, nothing more. What if she had actually found a man to go to her father and ask for her hand ignorant of the news? Sophie could hear her mother's voice even then: *No, wait dear man, you may have my daughter, but the sum that induced you as much as her beauty, will have to wait a little longer, since we've invested it. It is to be hoped there are no storms. . . .*

She was withdrawn from the London season the next day. No man, the likes of whom she had ever met, would ever take her under such circumstances now.

CHAPTER ONE

Kent, March 1814

Sophie pushed the spade in the half-frozen ground around the pink moss rose that needed to be moved. It was still months before the tulips, banksia roses, primroses, and bluebells fill the gardens of Rowengate Park, before the espaliered fruit trees against the walls, flowered and filled the air with their delicious scent. The garden hid the air of neglect about the hundred-year-old red-brick house that was the home of Benedick, the Right Honourable Lord Canmore, but when financial ruin falls upon a house, baron or not, there is little to hide the effects without going into debt. Trying to keep the garden from ruin alone though meant that even in earliest March there was work to be done.

How could Sophie forget the family's downfall? Her father could not sell Rowengate, but the sale of their London house had been enough to pay off all debts. What was left would keep them from bankruptcy, but none of it could be spent, not even the interest, so that the principal could grow. They had the house, cattle, poultry, crops, cheese, ale, cider, pigs, vegetables and fruit, so they wouldn't starve or be homeless. Slowly they would dig themselves out of the hole, but by that time, Sophie would be far too old to find a husband. When all was said and done, they were living on little more than £500 a year, the money from her mother's inheritance, and what goods the estate could produce for sale, little though there was left after all the needs of the estate were filled.

With three girls still at home, her brother Jasper had gone into the army, despite being heir to the barony, to lessen the burden on his parents. If Jasper had finished Cambridge, he might have made a better living. With the little money they could spare, he had purchased the cheapest commission available in the infantry and now, at the age of twenty-one, he was in the thick of the peninsular campaign against Napoleon, risking death every day. Since he had left to fight, his papa daily lamented the fact that he should have gone into the navy. They might not have seen Jasper for a decade, but at least he would have been in less peril.

The navy, which required no commission to join, was for second sons and men little better than prisoners. It was Papa's doing which had sent him there. As Jasper would be a baron one day, fortune or not, he was above those in the navy.

Without warning, Sophie felt her gypsy hat knocked off her head. 'Sophie, come away from there. No young lady does gardening. Pick some flowers for drying at least. Whatever would a husband say? Such a beauty and you do nothing to encourage them. With your skill at my mama's game pie, you should be setting a table to woo the entire county.'

Sophie lifted her eyes up to her mother with a sigh. For one thing it was March; not a flower to be had. Secondly, they only kept two house servants, a cook and a maid: they hadn't had a gardener for two years. Thirdly, she would keep her tongue about her mother's behaviour that had kept the men away. Sophie would have gladly been encouraging if one had shown an interest. Anything to escape her mother; even a poor man as a husband would be better than her existence now.

'No one will see me, and you know full well Mrs George is getting too old for it. Perhaps you would prefer it to be an overgrown wilderness when we do have a visitor?' Her mother's exasperated look was worth it. Sophie knew an ethereally blonde beauty looked incongruous tending the garden, but better that than every standard lost. It wasn't as if being caught with a spade in her hands was the same as being caught alone with a young man.

'It just so happens we do have a visitor. Your cousin Mariah is here to see you. More to the point, she has brought her aunt, the Marchioness of Sandbourne. Make yourself presentable and come and greet them.'

Sophie stood and brushed the leaves from her old serviceable gown. Her mother rushed around and undid her apron before pushing her in the direction of the house, as if that would improve her appearance before a marchioness. She wore the cheapest fabric that couldn't be called peasant worthy and had decorated it well, hem and neck, with embroidery. By village standards she was well dressed, by town standards, well, she tried not to laugh.

Sophie caught sight of Lady Sandbourne on the Beauvais tapestry-covered sofa, a vibrant reminder of their past fortune and certainly the most expensive piece left in the house. Lady Sandbourne was a grand woman in pale-blue silk whom Sophie had met only once. Not yet forty, she was nonetheless widow to Gerald Armitage the Marquess of Sandbourne. She was still a handsome woman. Mariah had told the story of her coming out many years before. Demaris Winters had her pick of no less than two barons, five viscounts, three earls, and a handful of the richest commoners in England despite being the daughter of a common brewer. Then again, brewers wealthy enough to be able to endow their daughters with £50,000 had little trouble marrying them off. After her father's turn of fortune, Sophie knew she had the ghastly sum of just one hundred pounds settled on her.

Everyone curtsied to each other as they entered the room. Sophie couldn't help but notice the look Mariah gave her aunt at the sight of her. The apron had not kept all the dirt from her dress. 'I do believe Sophie had the right idea. It is such a lovely day after this dreadful winter. Why don't we take a turn in the gardens?' Cousin Mariah was an approachable girl whose laughing brown eyes kept her audience enthralled. Her aunt was like a fine piece of art. Yet most would agree Sophie ranked finer then either in looks.

'Excellent idea, Mariah. It will surely be

welcome after such a long carriage ride too,' Lady Sandbourne announced. She fell in next to Lady Canmore, leaving the two younger girls to follow some distance behind.

'This is an unexpected visit,' Sophie broached, as soon as the older women were out of earshot.

Mariah looked ahead to see that they were quite alone and a smile spread across her square face. 'I have business with you, and I don't want your mother to hear.'

Her laughing eyes sparkled so it was not dire news at least. 'What possible business could you need to see me about? A social call I can understand.'

'My aunt is taking me to London for the season.'

Sophie felt her heart fall. 'Oh, is she indeed? That's wonderful, Mariah.' She tried to sound cheerful.

Mariah was no silly girl though. She stopped and turned to Sophie with a questioning eye. 'I deserve no censure if you think I came to you with the news after the change in your situation. My aunt is offering to take you as well.'

This was almost worse, a pity season. The only thing that appealed to her was that if she said yes, she would be out from under her mother's thumb. One look at the gown Lady Sandbourne wore though was all it took to remind Sophie of her plight.

'Thank her kindly but we can't afford to buy clothes grand enough for a season, not in her circle. I'd look no better than a governess hanging on someone's sleeve.'

Mariah's eyes sparkled with a humour Sophie didn't feel herself. 'That's why I said I have business. She's offering a trade: your father's barouche is just sitting there — the use of it for the season in exchange for clothes enough to see you through the season. We need your advice on how to broach it best. Almack's starts the second week in April. We've only a month for you to get enough to wear.'

Escape at last. 'Mariah, may I hug you?' Sophie didn't give her a chance to answer though.

Sophie watched the sun setting over the horizon. *Freedom!* The shades of purple and orange seemed brighter as they hit the clouds than they had the day before. The clouds were no different, but she was seeing with different eyes, eyes that were not bound to see that same view day after day without end.

'Sophie, may I see you in the library?' her

father asked, as the last rays faded from sight. Sophie followed him to his refuge, the lamps were not lit and only the fire gave out light. 'What exactly is the arrangement you have with Lady Sandbourne?'

'Whatever do you mean, Papa? Do you object to letting her use the barouche?'

Lord Canmore sank heavily into his chair before the fire. Sophie swore he had aged a decade in the last two years. He had practically gone grey in the two weeks she had been in London. 'You have borne this turn of mine most admirably. Never a complaint about going without the finer things you once had. Your mother sees only that you will have another chance. How much is Lady Sandbourne offering for the use of our carriage?'

Sophie turned to face the fire. She had given no promise, but still. . . . 'Mariah intimated that her aunt is in some difficulty herself, but she has dresses enough to be remade for me and we have a grand barouche to offer. The two of us, it seems, have this one season to change our fortunes by marrying well.' She hated to say it, watching her Papa flinch as the words came out of her mouth, but really there was no other option. She must marry well on her charms, or remain a spinster with the family in genteel poverty and her mother's hateful tongue. The house, while pretty, was no great estate. What was left of its productivity provided maybe a hundred pounds a year after the workers were paid. They had been living on the interest of their fortune earned at the height of the spice trade. Genteel poverty remained now, enough to live on, but, as peers, not enough to keep the ridicule away.

Sophie swore she saw a tear threaten to slip down her father's cheek. 'If you are lucky enough, secure a good man's favour. I will not have you married to an ass for the sake of security. I won't tell you not to go, only choose with your heart, not with thoughts of our situation. You are not desperate. You're nineteen, Daughter, not an old maid just yet. Choose well.'

'Oh, Papa.' She kissed his forehead softly. When she pulled away, she found close to fifty pounds in her hand. 'Papa, what have you done?'

'Lady Sandbourne may bestow kindness on you, but she doesn't have to think you a pauper. I was thinking you could take Anjanette Rutherford with you as well. She should see a little of the world.'

'You can't afford to give this,' Sophie argued.

'Your mother's annual sum is still intact and your brother sends a little when he can. He told me to buy cigars and brandy, but I could not treat myself to such while we live without so much. I saved it for a luxury and now it has appeared before me. Use your season well, Sophie.' He shooed her off to bed without giving her a chance to return the money or say thank you. *Use your season well,* the closest she ever heard her father admit that it was her only chance of escape. He was far more delicate about the matter than her mother was.

Walking up the stairs, Sophie knew she had little hope of marrying well or otherwise. Resolving not to speak of her situation in London, she would enjoy her stay regardless; it might be the last.

Sophie still lay in bed staring at the ceiling above her. Could she actually be free from her mother's tongue for a whole summer? Delightful silence, and nothing more disagreeable than attending parties and balls with the rich of London. Once she was one of them, now a guest, but to get away she didn't care. A knock on the door broke her contemplation.

'Yes?'

'It's me, Miss Sophie,' announced a soft,

clear voice in answer.

Sophie pulled on her robe as the door opened to reveal Miss Anjanette Rutherford. The darkest jet lashes surrounded her emerald green eyes, while auburn hair framed her striking face. They had never been close, though she was an amiable, sweet girl. Older for one, and Mama had considered her an undesirable connection. A baron and a solicitor did not mix.

'Lady Canmore sent word that you were in need of a lady's maid for a season in London. I thought I might come and learn your routine before we reach Town. There needn't be any bother then once we get there.'

Sophie felt her heart fall to hear such words. She had thought her father meant as a companion, for Miss Rutherford was Papa's solicitor's daughter. If Mama was the one who had sent the message though, there was no telling what had been said. The family wasn't without funds, just not wealthy, just not fashionable as if he had been a barrister. In other words not high enough society for Mama. 'A lady's maid? Heaven forbid, I'd never know what to do with one. You can gladly come as a companion, there is ever so much to see. I know I can't invite you to the balls and such, since

I myself am only to go as the guest of another, but to trap you in the house the entire time just seems cruel. Would that suit, Miss Rutherford?'

Never a more genuine smile had Sophie seen.

CHAPTER TWO

Riding through the bustle of London, Sophie had forgotten just how busy it was even without society about. It was still early, hunting had not just finished in the country, though not long enough ago that everyone had made it to Town. Mariah needed dresses, as did Sophie, even if Mariah need not make do with remade handmedowns. In the middle of Mayfair, the most fashionable neighbourhood in town, the barouche pulled up in front of what could easily be called a palace. Why had Mariah said her aunt was in financial difficulties? The pale golden stone glowed in the sun as liveried footmen assisted them out of the barouche. Her country clothes stood out all the more to mark her in these settings. With the bedroom door eventually shut behind her and a handsomely appointed green-decorated room before her, she hoped no one had heard her sigh. She was sure there wasn't a piece to be seen that she could have purchased with her mother's entire annual sum.

'Shall I unpack your trunk?' Anjanette asked.

Lud, it would be a very long summer if she couldn't have a thought to herself. It seemed as if Mama was reaching from afar to rob her of the little peace she might have found away from her.

With the Marchioness's old wardrobe laid out on a green chaise, Sophie could only stare. It was large indeed, but it was also out of date: longer sleeved gowns from the turn of the century, what had to be French-styled gowns, as much more of her bosom would show than allowed for a proper young lady, but oh, the fabric was wonderful. Silver and gold-embroidered, silk velvets, the finest lace, and muslin. A few perhaps might need only the sleeves shortening and a fichu, but most . . . Mariah was calling on an acquaintance leaving Lady Sandbourne alone to hear Sophie's groan.

'Come, my dear. Let's take the carriage and visit the shops. That one you're holding would look spectacular with a fine muslin overdress I think,' Lady Sandbourne announced pulling on her gloves. Being a brewer's daughter, she was no snob, despite her rank. Sophie had no feeling that the marchioness condescended to have her around, peer's daughter or not. That would have been too much to bear.

Sophie lifted her head. 'You knew the dresses were in this state when you made the offer? It will take months to adjust them all.' She was finding it difficult not to show her anger. This was exactly the reason she had refused in the first place. Rather a poor miss with her scant pride intact than fuel for the London gossips again.

'Sophie, my maid, Inviolata, has been seeing to my wardrobe for years. She was one of the best mantua-makers in France before the Revolution. She made all you see here and she can remake them all, equally well, and in far less time than you fear.' Lady Sandbourne picked up her hand and squeezed it comfortingly. 'We shall go to the shops and see what ladies are wearing, see the newest fashion plates. Perhaps buy some fabric that is all the crack, then we will bring it back and create splendour. I promise, you will not be ridiculed. A face as pretty as yours can always overcome a lack of fortune if the man is rich enough. I should say a man with ten thousand pounds a year at least.'

Sophie lifted her gaze to the handsome woman who held her hand. 'Why did you deceive me to get me to come? With this house, you can't be in trouble enough not to afford a barouche of your own. I know I shouldn't ask such impertinent questions —'

Lady Sandbourne laughed, not a silly giggle, a full out laugh. 'I made the suggestion of a trade to save your poor parents' pride. If Mariah implied otherwise, then I am sorry. You shall ride in the fine barouche you call your own. I will empty my house of dresses I no longer wear and Mariah will have a friend with her during this dreadful marriage hunt. My sister was prepared to bring Mariah herself, but I dare say it would have been the same as your own mother if she was able to bring you to Town. I could not see either of you left to such desperate chaperons, not if I had the means to prevent it. I shall see you both married well before season end, on my honour. You've already been presented at Court so you've a start on your cousin. You need not worry about that detail.'

Sophie lowered her eyes. 'Mother might be desperate, but Father — I think he wishes to prevent me from ending up as he did with Mother — affection perhaps, but love, I do not see that he has that. Papa will not give his consent if I choose just for a fortune.'

The corner of Lady Sandbourne's mouth curved up. 'Well then, we shall just have to make sure you fall soundly in love with an excellent man of good fortune. Do you care for a particular title? It will help me narrow down my search.'

Sophie could only gape as Lady Sandbourne turned to leave.

Despite all the talk of Sophie's situation, it was her connections that Lady Sandbourne would not refuse for dinner the very next night. An old friend of her father's, Rhys Dyson, sent the invitation the very day she arrived. For the occasion, Lady Sandbourne pulled out a gown of her own of the newest style for Sophie to borrow.

'I know I'm not here as maid, Miss Greenwood, but Lady Sandbourne's woman seems to be very busy with your cousin's wardrobe. If you like I have a good hand with a needle; I could get some things done quickly when I'm staying behind. I know I would hate being taken everywhere knowing that I wasn't up to scratch.'

Sophie let out a sigh of relief. 'Oh thank you, Anjanette.' For a moment Sophie smiled, and then what she was saying sank in. 'Aren't you coming with us this evening?'

'Lady Sandbourne made no mention of it.'

'No, I insist you come. It's my invitation not hers and since it is to Mr Dyson's home that we are going, you must see your father's old friend. If I did not take you and it was found out, your family would be most put out.'

Anjanette smiled faintly. 'Very well.'

On the carriage ride, a face suddenly appeared in the window scaring poor Mariah. By the time the others had turned round though, he was gone.

'Well, what did he look like?' Lady Sandbourne demanded.

'How should I know? Like any vagabond might.' Mariah almost screamed, still frightened by the unexpected face.

Only as they pulled up to the house did Sophie remember that Rhys Dyson was the now richest man in half of England. He'd been a well off but not a rich merchant when she had last seen him. No wonder Lady Sandbourne didn't scoff at the acquaintance.

'Ah, Sophie, I'm so glad you could came.

I wasn't sure that you would at such short notice,' the very man himself called, as they alighted. Not his footman, or butler greeted them, he did. He was a tall man and, despite his age of sixty-odd he still stood 6'7' with a bright shock of white hair. 'And who are your companions?'

Lady Sandbourne sniffed; it was an easy guess that she didn't like not being introduced immediately and in favour of an impoverished nobody at that. 'My hostess, Lady Sandbourne, my cousin, Miss Mariah Randolph, and another old friend from Kent, Miss Rutherford.'

'Wonderful. Not to slight my beautiful guests, but this was to be a night for men only until my guest of honour failed to arrive on dry land. We have heard there is a storm hampering his arrival. In the same post, I received word that you've come to Town. I couldn't wait a moment longer to invite you to dine since my original plan had gone awry. Come in, come in.'

If Sophie thought that Lady Sandbourne's house was a palace, she changed her mind after one look at her surroundings. Her hostess had a hovel compared to the lavish furnishings they were amongst now. Introductions were made, most of them to men of whom she knew nothing, and they proceeded to produce enough compliments that Lady Sandbourne didn't even notice Mr Dyson draw Sophie and Anjanette aside.

'Come to the library for a while; I should like to hear how you two are faring. I trust you both are in good health?'

Sophie hadn't seen her host in some years; she couldn't have been more than twelve when he was often in their lives. It was somewhat of a surprise that he was still so interested in her welfare.

'Now, my dears, tell me all the latest news.' He announced as he seated them near him. Only as Sophie sat could she look him even near eye-to-eye.

'My father would have surely sent his regards if he had known we were to see each other,' Anjanette said. 'He's often spoken of you when your name was mentioned in the newspapers.'

Mr Dyson tented his fingers to rest his chin on them. 'Yes, I haven't seen your father much since I had to change solicitors when my business interests were conducted more in London. And you, Miss Green-wood? Is your family in health?'

Sophie took a deep breath. She knew Anjanette had heard all the gossip. 'I suppose I shouldn't mince words, but tell you that Father lost almost everything two years ago.'

Mr Dyson's head nodded faintly. 'Truly so bad. He hadn't told me the amount he put into our venture would leave nothing if it failed.'

Sophie couldn't hide the gasp. 'You were part of it?'

'We dined together and I talked of commissioning a ship to head east for spices. Several days later he came to me with the money. His brother was to captain the ship. I was in Jamaica when it sank, and I saw nothing of your father when I returned. I thought perhaps he had sailed off too.'

A servant brought them each a glass of wine, something her mother would hardly allow when she was at home. 'No, he sold the London house to pay off his debts before anyone could come and do it for him. He's not been back since then.'

Mr Dyson settled back in his chair with his own glass and a smile grew. 'Sophie, I expected you to arrive with a husband. We were across the room when you were presented and I did not have a chance to say hello, but I have to say I expected you to marry within weeks.'

Sophie couldn't help the bitter laughter from forming. 'No, it seems without my knowledge part of the money taken for your venture was my portion. They sent me to

Town believing it would be replaced before it was ever needed. When the ship went down, Mama went to half the men in the county trying to push a match before anyone knew the money was gone. Now she's spent two years treating me as if I was the one to blame for its loss.'

Anjanette looked away; Sophie swore she saw a tear slipping down her cheek, but for what though? It was her family's scandal; the Rutherfords remained untainted.

He simply stared at her, his face turning redder as each moment passed. 'Child, if I had known, I never would have let them join in the venture with me. I made my own fortune. I know full well that not everyone has the privilege of such resources.'

Anjanette let her talk on without interruption.

'Papa took a risk and it failed. If the ship hadn't sunk, he could have pushed for a long engagement if I had found a match quickly and there wouldn't have been a difficulty. A second season, like most, to find a husband, and the money would be there without anyone knowing. The blame I have is for Mama; she was trying to trick men into an engagement where there was no hope of ever providing the dowry. What if she had succeeded? We could have been sued, in addition to the scandal it would cause. And what of me? What if I had actually been married to a man who subsequently found out everything was a lie? Can you imagine what torment I'd have to live with had she succeeded? I'm surprised you even invited me, others hardly deign to have me in the same room.'

Mr Dyson snorted. 'Why? Because you're poor?'

'Because Mama is a fortune hunter and that makes me one as well, doesn't it? I found all this out after it happened and yet I'm tainted.'

'Dinner is served, sir,' the butler announced at the door.

Mr Dyson held out his arms for Sophie and Anjanette to take. 'You make me feel guilty. I feel I should replace your portion, Miss Greenwood.'

That brought a true laugh as they made for the door. 'Why should you, Mr Dyson? Mama would hate to hear this, which is probably why I am saying it. Then I would attract a man who cared only for money enough to overlook the scandal. Of me, he would care not one whit. I'm afraid after seeing my mother's true colours and my father's reaction to them, I am resolved not to make such a match. Therefore, I am also resolved to leave London in the autumn and return home a spinster. I have a summer free of Mother's nagging. Miss Rutherford comes as my companion, though Mother thinks her my maid — perhaps escaping my mother as well.' Maybe she was right when she caught a gasp from Anjanette's direction.

'Sophie, child, I can't believe you said such a thing. You certainly have grown up more than I should have imagined.'

'Ah there you are,' Lady Sandbourne called out as they returned to the others. 'See what I mean, gentlemen? Is Miss Greenwood absolutely not the most divine creature? I'll have her married off by summer's end, mark my words. Don't you agree?'

'She's been like this since I arrived. Mark my words I shall have a case of nerves if she keeps it up,' Sophie muttered, only loud enough for Mr Dyson and Anjanette to hear.

His laughter filled the room and Anjanette tittered behind her hand. 'Dinner everyone.' As Mr Dyson led the way into the dining-room, he was rather quiet. 'You must let me do something,' he said eventually, as Sophie was seated at the elegant table. They were a little apart from the others so no one heard his offer.

'Send Papa some cigars and brandy then. He sent what funds he had free for me to use. Maybe a new dress for each of my sisters? I have Lady Sandbourne's hospitality and cast-off clothes, so I'll be living quite well. They are doing without. We are well taken care of for essentials, but there hasn't been a luxury in the house in two years.'

'And what of Jasper? What should he like as a treat?'

At the thought of Jasper, she sobered. She could see his pleasant countenance even then. 'He bought a commission in the 77th Infantry. It's all we could spare. He's in the Peninsula, the last we heard, chasing General Bonaparte. I imagine he would only like to come home.'

Mr Dyson shook his head. 'You're a good girl, Sophie.'

Lady Sandbourne interrupted and asked some trifling question and that was all Sophie was able to say to him for the rest of the evening. Lady Sandbourne made Mariah and Sophie change places and kept trying to force the man next to Sophie to engage her in conversation. Lord Rivington was quite a bore. He looked down his nose at her and instead spoke to Mr Dyson. Sophie could not care less about making a match, but it would really try her nerves if not one person would even talk to her.

CHAPTER THREE

There followed days of Inviolata fitting her dresses and yet nothing really to wear, of leaving cards with old acquaintances, many of whom she knew would never receive her or return the visit, seeing family and days of riding in the park. Until after Easter, there wouldn't be the whirlwind of events, just the occasional dinner and a dance.

Sophie took out one of Lady Sandbourne's beautiful bay hunters while the others were still in bed, yet again. She was dressed in a deep-green riding habit, one of the few dresses that had been deemed worthy for her to wear due to Anjanette's deft handiwork. Everything belonged to Lady Sandbourne, from the gown to the horse. Only the thoughts between her own two ears could be called her own. She fitted the part she played, but it was only that, a part, as if she was an actress upon the stage, or in this case, Hyde Park.

The horse reared suddenly, breaking her out of her thoughts as she landed firmly on her bottom. Sophie watched the hunter take off for parts unknown. A man in livery ran after it as another helped her up.

'Are you injured, miss?' a gentleman asked, as he came down from his carriage. He put her in the awkward position of bowing when she was unable to return it.

'I don't know what happened. I think no harm was done other than a sore limb or two.' Her eyes scanned for a child who had been throwing stones perhaps. Her mind might have been on other things, but she had heard something just before she fell so ungracefully. There was a rather dishevelled man laughing, but who wouldn't at the sight of her sprawled like a fool?

'I'll see you home. James can bring the horse after he catches it,' the gentleman announced.

Sophie looked up. Perhaps in his forties, as his temples were starting to grey, but overall he was a handsome man with fine clothes, to be sure. An empty carriage alone with a man, though, sore backside or not, would never do. 'No, I'm not far away. When the horse is recovered, it can be returned to the Marchioness of Sandbourne's residence in Mayfair.' Then a face appeared out the window of the carriage, familiar at once and yet not the same.

'Do get in, Sophie. My husband is only following my orders. You have as fine a riding seat as any I've known: it's not like you to part company.'

'I thought I heard something strike the horse, if I hadn't been lost in thought I imagine I would have been able to control him.' Sophie smiled at the striking redhead with pale translucent skin and eyes green like the grass. 'It's been two years, Phillippa. What happened to you?' *What had happened?* She had married very well indeed judging by her carriage and clothes. They had been thick as thieves once, learning French and Italian, among the other graces from Sophie's tutor, until Phillippa's father, a barrister, had inherited an entailed estate in Surrey. As he was fifth in line, it came as an unexpected windfall. They had been apart for some years but they had come out together. They had giggled with delight as they shopped for just the right ribbon or bonnet. Then Sophie had grown up overnight. They were of an age when she was taken home from London two years earlier but she felt far older than the Phillippa she saw now.

Phillippa giggled. 'Me? You were the one

who vanished. Do you not even read the announcements? I married Mr Everard Beresford MP last summer. We met some time after you last left London,' she replied, opening the door of the carriage. Mr Beresford, himself, held it open as Sophie climbed in. After all, one of his men was running after her horse.

Sophie could only stare at Phillippa as she sat down and Mr Beresford found his place beside his wife. 'I would have come if I had known of the wedding! Not even a letter?'

Even at his age Mr Beresford blushed; Phillippa lowered her eyes. 'We eloped. Papa wished me to marry the man whose land bordered ours. Kathryn would have killed me if I had followed Papa's order. She'd been in love with our neighbour for years. At last, Papa forgave me as they became engaged recently now that she is of an age to marry. Now that you are back, we shall just have to find some man to run off with you. You'll have something to tell one day.'

'Two years later, I still get ill looks when I am introduced to new acquaintances. Mama made even that almost impossible.' Sophie tired of the topic yet again as Phillippa nodded. The mainstay at home, she hardly knew of another topic to speak of. It was no wonder she hid in the garden most days and took long walks. She and Phillippa whispered of the little they knew of the scandal before she was taken home from London. That was the last time they had spoken. 'Anjanette Rutherford is here with me. You remember her, I imagine?'

'Of course; Mr Rutherford and Papa spoke often during the course of business, but I'm little acquainted with the daughter. She is older than us, is she not? Often with her aunt I believe Papa said.'

'Jasper's age yes. Was there an aunt? Mama never let us speak much.' Only saying it out loud made Sophie set her mind to the matter, that her papa was concerned about Miss Anjanette Rutherford seeing some of the world when Sophie herself had not spoken more than a few words to her until this season. Papa knew the father, but he hadn't known Anjanette more than a little. Why would he have suggested it at all?

Mr Beresford had been watching her as she spoke. Her words made him smile, which was almost as much of an insult as the ill looks others gave her. 'I think, my dear, we should introduce her to Mr Knott.'

Sophie tried to hide a groan. There had been no communication between them for two years and now even her friend believed she could marry her off in a mere three months. 'Not another matchmaker. Lady Sandbourne has her hand at that task already.'

'No,' Phillippa smiled. 'I think our task is to amuse Miss Greenwood. Leave the matchmaking to the more adept. I dare say we shall not mention the name of any eligible young men, no matter how foolish and rich, who might take Sophie without a farthing. And Mr Knott is surely both.'

Mr Beresford's laugh filled the carriage. 'Of course he is foolish. Who wouldn't be when your parents name you Jason Argo Knott.'

Phillippa linked her arm in Sophie's as they sat there. 'There will be enough nights for Lady Sandbourne to do her magic. We are going to the opera in a few days. I insist you accompany us and perhaps take dinner with us one night next week. You won't be thought such a fortune hunter if you aren't on the husband hunt every evening and I long to talk to someone other than my husband's old gentlemen friends. Once a week, we'll dine together until we return to the country; I insist.' Sophie caught the wink that Phillippa gave her husband though.

'I'm not as badly off as all that. I have a hundred pounds settled on me and fifty in my reticule,' Sophie joked, adding to the conversation. It was pure delight not to be surrounded by the serious talk of marriage. It had been so long since she had just laughed, even at herself.

'Speaking of the country, do you suppose Lady Sandbourne could do without you for Easter?' Mr Beresford asked. 'I'll have business to attend to while we are back at Coverly Court. With my wife wanting your company so much, I don't think she'll complain if you came to Coverly Court.'

Phillippa's face lit up. 'Oh yes, I heartily agree with that. I have missed you, Sophie. You must come for Easter.'

Back inside the house, Mariah was just coming down the stairs. 'Already home? Aunt told cook another half-hour before breakfast. I'm glad though, you can help me decide what to wear to the first ball at Almack's. I don't wish to match you with Inviolata doing both of our wardrobes.'

'I'll be at the opera that evening. Wear whatever you wish.'

'Oh, who invited you?' Mariah asked disappointed.

'I ran into Phillippa Condiff. You remember her, she was often at our house some years ago. She's married to Mr Everard Beresford now. I've been invited to go to the country with them for Easter too.'

'Mariah! Sophie!' the marchioness called. 'Do get dressed. As soon as we've eaten, we really must make some calls. I've just heard that my neighbour, Lady Naismith, has her nephew to stay. I met the boy some years ago and if his potential has come true, he will be a most agreeable dance partner.' Mariah rushed up the stairs, her unarranged hair flying behind her.

'I've been invited on Wednesday evening of each week to accompany Mrs Beresford. Her husband is a Member of Parliament,' Sophie announced, adding on his position just to stop any arguments about their suitability, as her hostess's eyes widened.

'You knew the patronesses at Almack's have declined to give you a subscription for their dances that evening?'

Sophie straightened her back. She had thought as much, but to hear it spoken plainly still stung. 'I suspected it. It was there, after all, that the news reached me of both my father's turn of fortune and my mother's subsequent behaviour. I did not expect that they would forget such a thing.'

Then the marchioness did something Sophie did not anticipate: she started smiling.

'You have more steel in you than I thought. You don't think you'll find a husband, do you?'

'When everyone thinks me the worst catch in the country, I have little hope of an offer. After two years of my mother berating me for her own actions, this is escape. I have had no invitations even to visit in two years. Now you claim you will find me a husband in one season, one with ten thousand pounds a year, no less.'

'My dear, if I can find a marquess then I have no doubt of my ability to find you the escape from your mother that you so desire.'

'With fifty thousand pounds as you had, my mother could be Medusa herself and no one would care, but for one hundred pounds? No, I will enjoy my time away from home before I am required to go back.'

Lady Sandbourne paused for a moment. 'Go and get changed. I've almost a mind to push you towards my son, but the lad's only fourteen. I would like a daughter with some backbone to her.'

Sophie collapsed on the chaise in her room even though much of it was still covered with the dresses to be made over. How would she endure the summer when everywhere she turned those she met kept throwing her past in her face?

'I have a dress finished if you would care to try it on?' Anjanette said quietly.

Sophie turned her head to the corner where she found Anjanette holding a gown of white silk trimmed with a simple maroon detail crossing over the low cut bodice. Dozens of tiny buttons ran down the skirt. It was simple and yet more elegant than the pile she lay on now. 'Isn't it delightful? Surely you'd like to wear it yourself after so much work.'

'I've nowhere to wear it, Miss Greenwood. I should like to pay some calls, but a gown such as this isn't required.'

'Anjanette, we hardly said a word to each other before this trip. I ran into Phillippa Condiff in Hyde Park. She thought there was an aunt with whom you spent much time and that was to blame for us not knowing each other well.'

Anjanette's hands fell to her lap, her jet-black eyebrows knitted in . . . *was it annoyance?*

'I don't wish to offend; you needn't answer me at all.'

'There was an aunt, since passed away, whom I helped to take care of, but that was for no more than a year. I have been less than a mile from Rowengate these last five years. Your mother thought I wasn't a suitable connection, that's all. A fine enough maid it seems though.'

'You must make this a season of your own to remember. You must pay all your calls. A companion is there to make life entertaining and, if you are happy, I shall be greatly entertained. One of us should be happy.'

Anjanette looked at her oddly just before there was a knock on the door. 'Are you ready to go, Sophie?' Mariah asked.

'Let me help. You'll be ready soon enough,' Anjanette murmured.

Why did Sophie feel as if she was being pitied just then? 'Go, make your calls.'

Sophie watched Lady Naismith flinch when they were introduced and hardly a word was said to her during their visit. Her nephew, a Mr Fraser, was most attentive to Mariah though. Tall, amiable, with correct opinions and fine manners, Mr Fraser, at perhaps twenty-five, was as fair as Mariah was dark. Sophie just sat there, mute, since no one spoke a word to her. The entire afternoon was a blur, Sophie couldn't even say what was said among the niceties that poured forth.

'Sophie, isn't Mr Fraser everything a man should be?' Mariah gushed, as they left their neighbours' house.

'The season hasn't even started yet. Are you going to fall in love with every man who flatters you?' Sophie snapped, and Mariah just gaped at her. She hated herself for saying it; she knew it was uncivil, and yet she couldn't keep the jealousy from showing.

'He asked me for the first two dances the opening evening at Almack's and dine with him and his aunt tomorrow,' Mariah offered, blushing as she did so.

'Even better,' Lady Sandbourne told her niece.

'His estate is in Scotland, though,' Sophie pointed out, at all their planning.

'And if she should secure him, Sophie, many will gladly visit for the pheasant shooting. She won't be sent into obscurity.'

Sophie realized though that it meant Mariah would be out of reach to visit, unless charity provided her carriage fare. Mariah was one of the few who had called in her exile. She would lose a friend for sure.

Dreaming of dinner with Mr Fraser, Mariah rushed to her room to find the perfect dress.

'Don't forget, Mariah, we need to pay a call on my sister this afternoon. Don't start getting ready for tonight just yet,' Lady Sandbourne called after her. Taking off her gloves, she turned on Sophie. 'What has caused your ill temper suddenly?'

Sophie was away from home; it was enough, ignored or not. She kept telling herself that anyway. Lady Sandbourne levelled her eyes before she smiled at her.

'There's hardly anyone in Town at the moment. Let her have her fancies with young men who'll dance with her until the assembly rooms fill up. She'll forget him soon enough when other men start clamouring for her.' Her words faded away as she gazed at Sophie. 'Never a word until Scotland was mentioned. . . . Ahhh! I see your worry now. Roberts!' she called to the butler. A few words under her breath and the stately man slid away.

Sophie removed her gloves and coat, giving it no real thought. Her mother was far from London and it would vex her exceedingly to know she was not looking for a husband. Sophie suppressed a smile just as something was pushed into her hand.

'What's this?' Sophie asked, as she opened her hand. A stupid question, for it was money, well, a bank draft at any rate. One thousand pounds stared up at her.

'Now don't think I'm giving you that to tempt a man. I still stand by my word to find you a man with ten thousand pounds at least. However, in case I fail, we'll see this in the bank this afternoon for you to use the interest so you may visit your friends without charity. That was your trouble, or I shall relinquish my claim of knowing people. Don't turn down the offer; it's small enough an amount for me and will stop you looking as if you had drunk a glass of vinegar at every man your cousin meets.'

Sophie couldn't help the smile coming. 'Indeed, it was my concern.'

Lady Sandbourne winked, completely ruining the staid impression she gave to the outside world. 'A little faith is all you need to find a husband. But a nest egg doesn't hurt one's morale.'

A little faith got her not one word during the evening with Lady Naismith and her nephew.

'Have you been in London long?' Sophie asked the man next to her at dinner, just to be polite. He was a large man with a rather menacing grimace on his face.

'No,' he muttered, before grabbing his wine glass. A little faith got her not more than one word with her companion at dinner either it seemed. Mariah, however, was half in love, so Sophie spent her time admiring the excellent harrico of mutton and almond cheesecake. The maid was the only one who spoke to her when she commented on the excellence of the cheesecake. A scrap of paper with the receipt was slipped in her hand as they were preparing to leave.

The maid winked. 'Don't tell her ladyship. She prides the house on that dessert.'

As they arrived at the marchioness's house, Roberts appeared with a package.

'Well, take it to my room. I'll open it later.' Lady Sandbourne waved him away.

'It is for Miss Greenwood, my lady.'

'Thank you, Roberts. It is rather large. Could you possibly have it taken to my room?' for which request she received a smile from the butler, but she had to endure a glare from Lady Sandbourne as they went upstairs. Eventually Anjanette closed the door to Sophie's room blocking her ladyship's glare.

'Who's it from?' Mariah asked eagerly.

Sophie couldn't help but smile, her cousin sometimes seemed so young. She ripped the paper quickly; it had been two years since she had had a present. Papa used to surprise them with little gifts but that had stopped very abruptly. 'The paper says Mr Dyson. What on earth can it be?' Inside one layer of paper at least lay a card: *If I'm delivering gifts to your family at your behest, I can't forget you as well. Jasper may just get his wish too.* Removing the last layers Mariah gasped when the contents were unveiled: a magnificent gown of silvery silk decorated with fine gossamer lace of a deeper grey hue. Therein lay another dress, too, it was for winter surely, made of deep maroon velvet. Sophie had mentioned a dress for her sisters, but this one was accompanied by a matching fur coat, muff, and hat, sable if Sophie had to give it a name.

Mariah kept caressing the softness.

How many times had she been told in the last weeks she couldn't go for a walk as she had in the country? Not without a chaperon at least. Even now, Anjanette walked alongside her as they went to pay a call three doors further down. Riding in the morning was about the only time she had to herself, all else was in the company of her host and cousin. That was fine, it was all the visiting they did that she found wearing: not being talked to, all but snubbed as she was given just enough attention to not label it a cut. People dared not provoke the displeasure of Lady Sandbourne, whose censure was better avoided.

Anjanette's cry was the only warning

Sophie had before powerful arms suddenly closed around her throat. Sophie could do nothing as she saw Anjanette hit the ground hard. A nasty voice filled her ears. 'Tell me where to find Greyfriars and you'll stay alive.'

The smell of the man was so bad it was something of a relief to be choked so that she couldn't breathe. 'I don't know what you're talking about,' she gasped out.

'Don't lie to me; I've seen you wearing your finery. Tell me where to find him.' His hands tightened. 'I've seen the letter. Tell me where he is!'

Just as she was about to run out of air, Anjanette finally found her tongue and started to scream. Sophie could suddenly breathe and sank to the ground as the sound of heavy, uneven footsteps ran quickly away. Strong hands helped her up as Lady Sandbourne and Mariah came at haste, along with most of the other residents of the street — their menservants at any rate.

'Get away from her, you blackguard,' Roberts, Lady Sandbourne's butler, ordered.

Sophie's voice strained, the words unable to form.

Anjanette spoke instead. 'He's the one who saved her.'

Turning to look at her saviour, it was no

wonder Roberts was sceptical. The man's strong jaw was covered in stubble, and tanned as few gentlemen are in England making his piercing blue eyes stand out all the more. Sun had bleached his dark hair and she could smell the sea on him. Somehow, she couldn't pull her eyes away from his.

'Thank you,' Sophie was finally able to whisper.

'You're sure he isn't the one?' Lady Sandbourne pressed.

Sophie shook her head forcing the words to come. 'The man who attacked me stank. I'm sure you can smell it even now on my clothes. It was not the sea I smelled.'

Her rescuer smiled faintly. 'Are you quite well? Nothing was stolen?'

A neighbour's servant sniffed disdainfully. 'Not from her, nothing to take.' The group broke up quietly, she was certain, so they could go report to their ladies how she made a spectacle of herself by being attacked.

Lady Sandbourne slipped in at her side fretting and clucking like a hen as Mariah helped Anjanette. 'I can't believe you were attacked outside my own home. Mayfair is supposed to be above that sort of thing.' Sophie was escorted away from her mystery rescuer before she could find out his name to thank him properly.

'Did you see the one who saved her? He looked as disreputable as her attacker must have,' Mariah announced once the door was closed.

Sophie saved her throat though Mariah's disdain was unfounded; she would stake the last of her reputation on that fact. He'd had a long sea voyage perhaps, and had just docked by the smell he carried. Not yet had time to shave.

'Fearful handsome, though,' Lady Sandbourne commented, leaving Mariah scandalized, not expecting such a thing from her aunt.

All Sophie could think of in order to forget almost being strangled was the look in the man's eyes. Even after it was mentioned she had nothing, those eyes had continued to smile at her.

CHAPTER FOUR

Sophie kept to her bed while people she hadn't seen in years suddenly started to pay calls. She was an entertainment. Not that her throat wasn't sore enough, she truly was ill. Ill, because every time she closed her eyes, hands felt as if they were closing around her throat. Ill, because the stench of him remained in her nose no matter how many flowers she asked the servants to bring. Ill, from staring at the bruises that dotted her neck. It was two days before she gingerly got ready for the opera. The evening was cool; the high neck of the fur coat that Mr Dyson had sent would hide the remnants of her ordeal.

'Miss, there was a letter for you just now. The man said it came from Canmore,' Roberts announced, as the bell rang at the door. Phillippa's face peered out of the carriage when the coachman led Sophie out of the house, the first truly friendly face she had

seen. Mariah had been too busy of late trying to catch the eye of the amiable Mr
Fraser even to notice her cousin.

'Miss Greenwood, are you being
followed?' Mr Beresford asked, after they
had made several stops for other carriages
along the way.

Her heart beat faster as the fear returned.
'Why would you ask that?'

'Just that I've been watching a man on
horseback since we left Lady Sandbourne's.
He seems to stop and go as we do.'

'Does he look as if he would smell?' She
asked.

Mr Beresford looked out the window
again quizzically. 'I dare say he does. No,
wait, now he's riding off. Why would you
ask if he smelled?'

Sophie peered out the window. No one
was in sight, no one to pay them any mind
at least. It was the first time she considered
herself the target of her attack. The two days
she had spent in bed, scared of her own
shadow, she had thought it was all a mistake.
Why would she be followed though? She
had no money or jewels to steal. The name
he demanded meant nothing to her. But if
she was being followed, could she still claim
mistaken identity?

'The man who attacked me is all I can

think of. Anjanette is hopeless at remembering anything. She was knocked to the ground and started to scream. By the time she could see, someone had run the man off. I didn't see him. I only know that he smelled dreadfully.'

Phillippa gasped in horror. 'You mean he's still following you?'

'I didn't think so, but perhaps he is.' That's what bothered her most. She had no clue who the man was, let alone where to find him. 'Whoever is Greyfriars?' She murmured to herself.

In the opera house, it was gloriously anonymous. They had arrived early, and asking Sophie's leave for a few moments Phillippa was soon busy speaking to a friend. The letter had been burning a hole in Sophie's reticule ever since she had read the name on it. Her father's writing was scrawled on the outside and it had been addressed to Lady Sandbourne's country estate. Her papa must have thought they had gone there first and it was just now catching up with her. Wrapped inside it though, she found one from her brother. She hadn't heard from Jasper for a long time and even this letter was dated months ago.

Dear Sophie

I don't know how to say this, but the house was broken into last night. Don't alarm yourself, we are all well, no harm done. I hate to think what might have been stolen, but the only thing I can find gone is the letter I received from Jasper, yours remains. Who is to tell with the mess that was made while we were out? I worry about your brother. The letter was filled with gibberish about some lad named Greyfriars to whom I should give aid if he ever came to me. He needed to be kept safe. I hope your brother hasn't taken it into his head to try to be a spy, as that's the last thing we need.

Papa

Greyfriars! What did Papa know of him? Sophie ripped open the second letter from her brother.

Dearest

I fear I cannot tell Mother and Father of my actions else they will condemn me for them. I cannot keep silent either as I fear I am being watched. After a fierce battle at Vitoria, our division broke through the French lines; it was a rout with far more French killed than we lost. You'll never imagine what we found. The French had abandoned their wagons and in them a fortune. Picton swears it's a million pounds in art, gold, jewels and money. I'm afraid it was too much temptation; instead of pursuing the French I filled my sack. Others went for the larger pieces, but knowing what I do, I found the best ones. Enough to undo all of Father's disaster. Suspecting that the colonel would see it all sent to England, I passed it on to our good friend Greyfriars so I could not be accused, but I think one of the men with me saw it. His own spoils were gone quickly through drunken gambling, so I can only presume he remembered what he saw and knows that I have not spent mine. I felt him watching me all the time and now he has deserted with strange talk of finding a fortune. That is also my reason for using Greyfriars as I would not put you in danger with the responsibility of such treasure. He will not betray me as he wants his share. It will be safe in England, and with it our family's fortune. You can retrieve it from him.

Farewell until I return,
Jasper

The fifty pounds she had from father, had

that been stolen too? It was the only thought that filled her head. Tears started down her cheeks and even a hand over her mouth could not hide the sound of her crying. Sophie sank on to the bench willing her legs not to collapse before she was perched properly. All she needed was one of the society matrons to see her sprawled on the floor in a final act of humiliation.

'Are you well?' a deep-voiced man asked quietly.

Startled, Sophie vaguely felt his presence, but she couldn't see him as her thoughts raced and her eyes swarmed with tears anew. Her brother was a thief and her attack wasn't a case of mistaken identity; it wasn't her imagination that she was being followed. As she became more distressed, he whispered, 'Close your eyes.' She tried to stop crying, but her sobs grew louder. He lowered his head closer to her ear. 'Close your eyes.'

It was the only command she could obey at the moment after such news, and she forced herself to comply. A soft linen handkerchief touched her cheeks wiping away the tears. Then a scrape of a door signalled someone else's approach; her public tears would be one more stick to add to the family disgrace.

'Sophie?' She recognized it as Phillippa's voice at least.

'I believe your friend is in some distress,' the man said.

Sophie did the only sensible thing she could, she fled, grabbing Phillippa's hand as she flew past. Outside, away from the bustle of patrons, she gulped in the cool night air.

'Sophie, what is wrong? Are you ill?'

Sophie shook her head slowly. It was about all she could manage. 'A letter was delivered just as we were to leave the house. You were engaged in conversation, so I read it. The news was not what I wished.' Opening her hand to show it to her, Sophie found not the letter but a soft linen handkerchief. *Lud!* She had grabbed the wrong thing in her haste; someone else would know of her disgrace.

'Jasper hasn't been wounded, or killed, has he?' Phillippa asked.

Her brother was . . . 'No.'

'Then come, the performance will keep your mind engaged elsewhere. It can't be as bad as all that.'

How could she tell her friend? Phillippa might forgive a loss of fortune, but a thief in the family was another matter altogether. 'My second season will end as quickly as my first,' she whispered to herself, as Phillippa pulled her back toward the theatre. Resting her eyes as the music started, Sophie sat bolt upright. *Greyfriars* — she had been so devastated that her brother had turned thief she had forgotten that one word. Did it come as any consolation that her brother was not a good thief? Not only had the man with him concluded he had the contraband, he knew where Jasper sent his letters even before they arrived. Her heart beat hard in her chest as she looked around. No, the man smelled too badly to gain entry to a box in the opera house. For the moment she was safe and then she caught sight of her rescuer from the street, who tipped an imaginary hat from across the way. He leaned over and spoke to . . . Mr Dyson. He had said his dinner guest was delayed due to a storm and the man in the street had surely smelled of the sea. Even in the dim light she could see he had obviously found a barber since she last saw him. Little of the sun-bleached curls were left. Sophie dipped her head in reply unwilling to cut the man who had saved her life, even if he wasn't a true acquaintance.

'He'd be a fine diversion, Sophie. He doesn't seem to mind that he found you crying at all,' Phillippa whispered.

'What?' Sophie gasped, and several

shushed her.

'Who could forget that face? If you weren't crying, you surely would know him on sight. He is not one to forget so easily.'

'That's the man who saved me from being strangled the other day. Do you know him at all?'

Phillippa raised an eyebrow. 'I saw my husband talking to him earlier. A business acquaintance, I believe. I've not yet met him socially.'

Sophie stared down at the handkerchief in her hand, in very fine embroidery she could make out the initials WK.

'Do you want an introduction? It could be easily done.'

'No.' Sophie paused a moment. 'No. I must not run after him. I would only prove every gossip right if I did that.'

After the opera was over, they hurried off for a late supper. The moment Sophie saw a man in the street, any man, the dread returned although nothing happened. Even in the carriage she wondered if someone was keeping watch, waiting to attack her once more.

'We leave for Easter in two days, don't we?'

'Yes, of course. Sophie, are you sure you're

quite well? That letter seems to have upset you terribly.'

'I would like to leave London. I'm too used to fresh air, I imagine. Two days will seem an eternity.'

'Quicker than if you were at home.' Mr Beresford teased.

The words shocked Sophie into laughing at least.

'Everard!' Phillippa chided playfully.

Her husband just stared at her. 'Did you just call me by my Christian name?'

Phillippa grinned devilishly. 'I have quite often, my dear. Just not in public.'

Sophie blushed at hearing them talking so intimately. Her parents hardly said a kind word to each other, let alone spoke as if they cared for one another. It wasn't just her father who would not give his permission to marry for a fortune alone, she would not give it herself, not if it would relegate her to a marriage like that of her parents.

After discovering out she was someone's target, even the simple pleasures she had were taken from her. Riding, the one time alone she had during the day, was snatched from her in fear of the man coming after her. Her salvation came when suddenly Mariah got up early enough to go riding with her. Why she had changed her habits was a mystery — at least until Mr Fraser rode up.

'Hello there. Miss Randolph, Miss Greenwood, fancy meeting you here. I should have been more faithful in my exercise if I had known I would have such company.'

Thankfully Sophie didn't have to hide the fact that he had seen and ignored her as he truly hadn't been out before, when she was at any rate. Sophie had usually ridden home before most made their way to the park. It wasn't that Mariah and Lady Sandbourne slept so late, only that Sophie got up so very early, an old habit to avoid her mother.

'Shall we ride together?' Mr Fraser asked.

'Delightful idea,' Mariah replied, moving closer to his side.

'Your aunt said your estates are in Scotland, I believe, Mr Fraser?' Sophie asked, as they put their horses to a walk.

'She must have meant my inheritance, Glensheen. Just last month some distant relation died and I inherited. I'm trying to get together a party to inspect it with us this autumn. Even if it's a shambles, we can hunt properly. I have an estate in Staffordshire where I actually live.'

'Stafford. Why, we're not more than ten miles from there,' Sophie answered with glee. With him being so near she could easily visit from Rowengate Park even without Lady Sandbourne's gift. Sophie smiled happily before she caught Mariah's glare. She almost laughed. Lady Sandbourne might discount Mariah's affection for Mr Fraser when others came on the scene, but no one seeing that look of jealousy would make such a rash statement.

Mariah chatted, hardly letting Sophie get a word in and when Mr Fraser moved away to greet an acquaintance, Mariah rounded on her. 'How could you?'

'I only asked, dear Cousin, because I didn't like the thought of you being so far off in Scotland while I was at Rowengate. You would be quite near for a visit, that was why I smiled. Mariah, he is the only man you have met so far. After Easter when Town fills, who knows who you will meet?'

Mariah suddenly looked older than her seventeen years as she realized the meaning behind Sophie's words. 'We met last autumn, Sophie. He had to leave on business for his mother and he's been in Ireland since then. No, don't look at me like that, no engagement was made. We haven't been hiding anything. Then it was nothing, but when we met again at his aunt's, I would say he shows true interest. I think he's finding people to join his party to Scotland so that there will be chaperons and I might be able to accompany him. Aunt Sandbourne heard of it, though, and I think she's under the impression he's trying to run away with me.' Mariah winked just before they noticed Mr Fraser coming back.

Chapter Five

Sophie climbed into the Beresfords' carriage and sank into her seat with a sigh. *Escape from her escape!* How tedious she sounded. At least for a week, someone would talk to her and by the time she returned all the hectic preparations for Mariah's presentation at Court would be over. At least for a week she would be away from London and the man pursuing her.

'I'm sorry, Miss Greenwood, there's another added to our party. I was to meet him at a neighbour's house where he was to be staying, but his host was obliged to stay in Town due to illness.'

'Not matchmaking, are you, Mr Beresford?'

Mr Beresford smiled crookedly. 'Well, if you're interested in expanding your holdings into sugar and rum, I'm sure we could arrange something. He's doing some land buying and selling.'

'For my hundred pounds, he'd probably sell me a chair.'

'Fine chair for that price though,' Phillippa quipped. Sophie laughed as they lurched to a start. Quickly it died when a menacing face forced its way through the window and then the stench filtered in through the windows. Seeing his face, Sophie grew even more fearful as it was the man she had seen laughing in the park. It also had to have been the face in the carriage window that Mariah had seen. He'd been following her about far longer than even she had thought.

'Tell me where Greyfriars is!' the man yelled.

Phillippa screamed and the man growled in annoyance at Mr Beresford's fist to his jaw before vanishing from sight.

'Miss Greenwood, whatever does he want?' he asked as he held Phillippa's head to his shoulder to calm her.

'My brother sent me a letter telling me where something is and he wants it.'

'It's with this Greyfriars?'

Trying to keep the tears from falling, her breath came short. 'Yes, only I haven't a clue who Greyfriars is. I don't rightly know what this thing is even. I can't tell this man so he'll leave me alone.'

'He doesn't look the sort to believe you even if you told him that you don't know.' A few moments of silence passed and Mr Beresford looked down to find Phillippa asleep on his shoulder, and the conversation ended. Sophie felt herself nodding off as well despite the rough road. The forty miles to Coverly Court went quickly, without having to stop at every rest along the way.

Sophie opened her eyes at Phillippa's nudge. She hadn't realized how much Jasper's news had upset her. The scandal was bad enough, but sleep had eluded her ever since hands had closed around her throat. One bruise was still covered with a scarf even after a week. Lady Sandbourne tutted sympathetically, but really had done nothing to help her feel better. No one had sent for the Bow Street Runners to catch her assailant. People were too busy gossiping to think about it, not that they were ghouls; it just gave them something out of the ordinary to talk about.

'Mr Kittridge arrived an hour ago, sir. He's been seen to his room, but presently he has gone to the village for a drink,' the butler announced, as he came out to meet the carriage.

'A drink? How odd, when we have enough

71

here,' Phillippa murmured.

'I'm sure our guest was bored here alone. He's earned his fortune, not rested on his father's laurels and interest.'

'Is that a kind way of saying he's in trade?' Phillippa asked.

'That's his kind way of saying I was trying to increase business with the local taverns, and am a mushroom,' a deep voice said behind them. Sophie turned and blanched — she'd found her rescuer. Shaved and perfectly dressed now, the most masculine man she'd seen in some time, he showed no proclivities toward being a dandy, his clothes being of very fine quality while looking far more like a soldier's only without regimental colours. Only his eyes truly looked the same, milk blue in his dark, tanned face and a smile that still didn't fade even though he must have heard the gossip about her by now.

'Mrs Beresford, Miss Greenwood, may I introduce Mr William Kittridge of Aintree.'

Sophie could only stare as he bowed slightly. Barely standing straight from returning his bow, Phillippa grinned devilishly.

'I believe you've met Miss Greenwood already though,' Phillippa said, not caring that Sophie glared at her.

Sophie gasped that he might think her ungrateful.

'Not socially, Mrs Beresford. I wasn't sure she wouldn't ignore me when we saw each other again at the opera.'

'Dear God, how can I ever thank you enough, introductions or not? I'll be forever in your debt.'

'Debt? Whatever are you talking about?' Mr Beresford asked.

'It was Mr Kittridge who saved me from being strangled. I didn't learn his name to be able to tell you of his gallantry. Lady Sandbourne rushed me off too quickly.'

Mr Kittridge held out his arm for her to take as the Beresfords entered the house. Sophie stiffened at him so near; he knew everything now, including her name.

'Shall we enter, Miss Greenwood? The cook promised me a spectacular dinner.'

Reluctantly Sophie took his arm as they followed the Beresfords into the house. They weren't shown to an inside room, but through to a wonderful enclosed grassy courtyard filled with centifolia rose bushes covered with pale-pink blooms. Pillared in worn stone, the house was older than Rowengate Park easily by 200 years. The barony of Canmore was only a hundred years old or so and Rowengate built then.

Peer, Mr Beresford might not be, but his family had held a place of distinction as gentry, at any rate, far longer than Sophie's had held the title. Sophie admired all the history around her, lived with, revelled in, not redecorated in the French style as so many had done. She tried to concentrate on the décor around her instead of the man at her side, one who could expose her scandal to the world with only a sentence. It was a beautiful house that Phillippa was able to run herself. There would be no house of Sophie's to run; she would remain under her mother's thumb, or some other just as bad. Inwardly, Sophie died a little when she realized Lady Sandbourne finding her a husband might be all that stood between her and becoming a companion. That really was the only option left. No, wait, what was she saying? She had already become a companion. She was Mariah's companion, brought to keep her cousin entertained while she looked for a husband. Sophie felt him draw near her again. Him; she spoke as if she knew Mr Kittridge when his name was the only thing she did know.

'Our hosts have retired to the garden. Shall we join them?'

Sophie looked around to find herself alone with Mr Kittridge. 'Oh, I drifted away in thought for a moment. I do hope you'll forgive me,' she mumbled, trying to hide her disquiet. How long would it be before he brought up the letter? The scandal it held?

'I'm sorry your original host is ill. It must have changed your plans a great deal.'

'I understand you know Mr Dyson. I find it odd that he was taken ill shortly after he found out that I could be staying with the Beresfords if not for his invitation. Did you tell him the party would be short a man?' He said nothing of scandal and thievery though and they went in to tea. Sophie felt her stomach lurch; he surely knew everything if he'd been speaking to Mr Dyson.

'Mr Beresford said you were in sugar and rum? Where is Aintree?' Phillippa asked, oblivious to Sophie's turmoil. After all, she didn't know what was in those letters he had.

'I was just off the boat from Jamaica the day I helped Miss Greenwood. Aintree is my estate there. We supply most of the rum to the Royal Navy.' All through supper, he told stories of the Caribbean to accompany the veal, beefsteak, sole, and a salmon pie. His voice . . . his voice not filled with the clipped tones of England, glided over her ears like a song she could never tire of hearing. Each new tale lulling to sleep the dread going on around her. No soldier, no smuggler, just a man with a family who owned ships and had sailed since he was a child. No bragging. He never mentioned it specifically, but reading into his stories, Sophie had to wonder if he had seen as much action as Jasper. Sitting across the table from him, every time Sophie lifted her eyes, Mr Kittridge was watching her, not staring or smiling stupidly. He was no love-struck boy, the looks were hard to place. Only when he caught her returning his look as she puzzled him out did a faint smile surface.

Sophie had almost forgotten the threat the letters held as nothing was spoken of them for several days, nor, as they went to church on Good Friday or Easter Sunday. After church though, Phillippa felt unwell, leaving Sophie to wander the woods of the estate unchaperoned, unfettered for the first time in weeks. The twig snapping behind her swiftly brought back the threat of a more serious nature than her reputation. Sophie could almost feel the hands at her throat again.

'Miss Greenwood.'

Sophie closed her eyes as she recognized Mr Kittridge's voice. 'Don't tell, please,' she whispered, not even sure he could hear her.

'I thought you might like your letters back in private.'

'What?' She turned suddenly. 'Private?' He held the letters out so simply. 'You read them?'

'A little hard not to as you left them fully open in my lap. It is no wonder your tears fell to hear of such news, especially after having been assaulted.'

Those eyes of his didn't show pity; she could not bear the thought of him staring at her as if she was nothing, like all the others. Tears threatened to fall again and Sophie ran, clutching the letters tightly this time. The path crunched beneath her feet as she rounded the house. Mr Beresford was emerging with his steward. A few steps more then a man stepped out from behind the garden wall grabbing hold of Sophie's arm through the closed front gate. His grip was unbreakable and, for the first time, Sophie got a good view of her assailant. Dirty blond hair almost covered his eyes; whether he was fair or ugly she couldn't tell with the beard covering all. A bath and a shave and he would be unrecognizable to her.

'You'll tell me where Greyfriars is, or I'll take care of you like I did your brother.'

'What have you done to Jasper?' Pulling

harder to break his grasp only made her arm hurt all the more as he added pressure. The bars kept him from going for her neck again but she was trapped as much as he was kept away.

'Miss Greenwood!' Mr Beresford yelled, as he saw what was happening. He started running with his steward and the yell brought Mr Kittridge around the corner of the house. All the men rushing to her aid but Sophie could only stare at the gaping hole in the man's leg, the source of the stench she encountered whenever he was near. She felt faint as the men pulled her free. Mr Kittridge was left holding a grimy coat as the man escaped and ran.

'Blast!' Mr Beresford cursed. The man was out of sight by the time they had the gate unlocked and open to follow.

'He said he took care of Jasper,' Sophie whispered. *Her brother gone, no, it couldn't be.*

'Your brother?' Mr Beresford looked out of the gate again at the empty lane. 'He wouldn't have run into that sort of man, would he?'

Mr Kittridge was already leading Sophie into the house, leaving Beresford without an answer. 'A glass of wine,' Mr Kittridge

78

told the maid as he helped Sophie into a chair.

'Petry, send word to the village now! I want a man on the gate within the hour,' Mr Beresford called as the events fully sank in.

'He can't have killed Jasper,' Sophie murmured again.

'Phillippa's alone!' Mr Beresford ran out of the room without another word.

No one said anything as the maid brought in a glass for her.

'I'd have the gardeners lock all the doors and windows, make sure the gate is secure,' Mr Kittridge told the maid at their host's rapid departure. Sophie felt him watching her as she took a drink.

'They don't know,' he stated, not asked, the moment the door closed.

Those words took away the tears and the anger surfaced. For the first time in years, she lost her temper. 'How can I tell one of my oldest friends my brother is a thief and the man who has been attacking me wants the spoils? I don't know who this Greyfriars is, and now he says he's killed my brother. Whom can I tell and not risk pulling them down in the scandal as well? I fear it would kill my father to hear of his heir's disgrace.'

'Calm down, Miss Greenwood. If you

keep shouting, everyone will know of your secrets.'

Calm down! You of all people tell me that? 'You know of them, isn't that enough?'

He smiled, the infernal man smiled. 'I'm a poor gossiper, no skill at *on-dits* at all.'

Anger, terror and rage inside her and Sophie had to force herself not to laugh, but a tiny giggle leaked through. 'None at all?' She had to ask it.

'None at all, so you see your secrets are safe. And if I haven't gossip to keep me busy, I shall just have to attend balls upon our return to Town and have mothers throw daughters at me.'

'I should say you are quite safe. They wouldn't want to send their girls off to Jamaica with all the slave uprisings there.'

Mr Kittridge sat back with his arms crossed watching her again. 'Mr Beresford can't be very good at gossip either. I have bought an estate on the coast in Somerset, and my business with our host is to purchase their London house. It is too small for their family, they wish to find another.'

Their family? Sophie let her gaze wander to the door where Mr Beresford had vanished, in such concern at his wife being alone — and Phillippa was ill this morning. *Sooner rather then later.*

'Might I be forward, Miss Greenwood?'

So polite, when she knew what was coming. 'How do you wish to offend?'

'I take it your loss of fortune was recent.'

'No, you really don't gossip, do you?' And here she was telling the whole sordid mess again. 'I embarked upon my first season without a farthing to my name it seems. My portion and my father's fortune were taken from the bank. He and my uncle, and it now seems Mr Dyson, concocted some scheme to triple their fortunes. A storm downed the ship though, with the money and my uncle. Then before I even knew of the disaster, Mama had visited half the eligible men in Town trying to marry me off without my dowry to back up her words. She said I still had my twenty thousand, but the news of the sinking had spread faster than she could visit and they already knew. Papa maintained respectability and his title by selling everything but the estate to pay his debts. If only Mama hadn't been so desperate, I might have actually married, despite it all. Not as well, but at least married.'

'There is only one word I can think of for that, ouch.'

No pity from him, but he understood the predicament she was in well enough and she was certain he had said it to make her laugh.

'I don't think very highly of your brother, Miss Greenwood. I will tell you that right now.'

'Can't you understand why he did it? Everything he grew up with is gone.'

'You mistake my meaning. I object to the grounds that he dragged you into this predicament. He sent whatever it is to this Greyfriars for safekeeping, but he must have been observed writing the letter to you and your father. Not the original, that letter was written well after Vitoria from what I read. Any sensible man might have just sent instructions with the box. But three dispatches, all of which might have been observed, is just foolish.'

Sophie laughed finally and watched his eyes rise as he drank from his own glass. 'You've never met Jasper. Even Papa would tell you I must have inherited his share of sense.' She knew he was distracting her from the fact her brother might be dead, that she could still feel the grip the man had on her arm. The laughter couldn't be kept in even with the thoughts of Jasper in the back of her head looming still. 'Have you a few secrets of your own, Mr Kittridge? For knowing of mine, you show a marked lack of concern.'

'What if I said the rum and sugar empire I'm living off was started long ago with privateer funds? Aintree was originally the name of the boat they used to sail the seas in search of Spanish gold. My ancestors had a sense of humour it seems. After that I wouldn't even consider what Jasper's done as stealing.'

'I'm shocked. Here I was expecting you to say you hadn't freed your slaves when the laws were passed.' Sophie expected his eyes to narrow but he only laughed.

'I didn't think women talked of such things.'

'Papa talks to me of a great many things when I've not escaped the house and Mama's tongue.'

'Then I'll stop watching my tongue around you, but if it will put your mind at ease, I haven't owned even one slave since before the laws were passed. My brother remains to run things there while I've come to run the business side here.'

At the knock on the door, Mr Beresford returned. Three men to guard them were placed about the house as luncheon was served.

She was up early and no one else stirred in

the house. Riding held little allure. The gardens in the courtyard held the early flowering roses. She couldn't contemplate a walk in the woods surrounding the house as she would have liked. The flowers' scent was delicious after the smells of London, but then rain drove Sophie inside. With no one around, she was able to explore. Everywhere she could see her old friend's work: pillows embroidered when they were younger, even a table they had both painted. The piano-forte held music from Phillippa's favorite composer, Mozart. Phillippa always complained she never played it as well as she liked. She'd preferred painting and drawing to practising the piano, while Sophie far excelled at piano and riding. Fingering the keys, Sophie wished she could stay at Coverly Court. Grand though it was, it felt like a home. She didn't feel comfortable in Lady Sandbourne's house in London. She was there to keep Lady Sandbourne occupied with finding her a husband almost as an entertainment. Was that Lady Sandbourne's vocation every summer? Was she bored with young ladies of good family with fine dowries and now needed the challenge of Sophie and her situation. The first notes of the sonata filled the room as she played and Sophie turned off her thoughts. No one was menacing her; her brother was safe; there was no scandal; there was just music.

'I should like to wake that way every morning,' Phillippa said, laying a hand on Sophie's shoulder. She still wore her wrapper, she truly had just woken.

'You are expecting?'

'How did you guess?'

'Mr Kittridge said you're selling your house in London as it was not big enough for your family and you've been ill most mornings since we've come away.'

'I'm not sure I'll be going back to London.'

Sophie stopped playing. 'Of course you won't. I only wish it could have been after the summer. How ever will I stand Town without you to make me laugh?' *How would she endure if Jasper were dead?*

'You might actually find a husband if you aren't with me all the time. You'll come this autumn, won't you? Once the season is over? I really did mean to be there longer, but I've been so sick lately. Mother says I'm far worse than she ever was with any of us.'

'If you invite me, of course I'll come. I'd be delighted.'

'Escape your mother a little longer too.'

'Well, yes, that as well.'

Phillippa sat on the bench next to Sophie.

'Play some more, Sophie, please.'

'Still haven't practised as you should?' she asked as the notes started to fill the room again.

'Did I ever?' Phillippa's eyes closed, just listening. When the page needed turning, silently it turned. The tanned hand at the page left no doubt as to whose it was, even without looking.

'Doesn't she play divinely, Mr Kittridge?' Phillippa asked, her eyes never opening. How did she . . . then Sophie caught the scent, earthy and exotic. Just the smell alone made her feel as if she was taken from staid England. She could still vaguely smell the sea on his clothes too. What had he seen? Where had he traveled?

'Don't stop playing, please.' Phillippa murmured just before she rushed from the room. No wonder they hadn't seen her most mornings.

'So many places you must have been.' Sophie murmured as she continued playing.

'What brings that up?'

'You smell of the world, Mr Kittridge.'

He smiled as he took a sniff of his lapel. 'My clothes were packed with bay rum leaves to keep them from smelling musty on the boat. My good clothes at any rate. I sup-

86

pose I should have everything washed even if they are clean.'

Did she dare say such a thing? 'No don't. It sets you apart from all the other gentlemen. I suspect you've come to improve your family name. It should help the ladies you aren't trying to capture overcome the pirated start to your fortune.'

'That would involve going to all those balls I've been far too busy with work trying to avoid.'

Sophie bit her lip. 'Then I pity them missing such an inducement. Turn the page, please, you seem to be getting distracted.'

Mr Kittridge grinned. No, he was shaking with silent laughter. A figure at the door caused Sophie to look up for just a moment. Phillippa watched her, a quizzical look on her pale face.

A knock on the door disturbed Sophie as she was dressing for dinner in her subdued beige room in the Georgian style. The whole house, while not remodelled with everything new, flowed together wonderfully. No one room stood out from the beautiful harmonious whole. Phillippa appeared with a gown in her arms.

'I'm not saying a thing about your situation, Sophie. I went to put this on for dinner and found it no longer fits. Would you accept it as a gift?' She held a gown of cream velvet that was absolutely divine. A Greek key pattern of gold embroidery edged it all.

'I can't possibly. It might not fit you today but may once the child has come —'

'I would hate for it never to be worn before it is out of fashion. By the time I am able to venture out, the dress would be out of date no doubt.'

Sophie felt it gently, the fabric was the softest she'd ever felt, even among those of Lady Sandbourne. Surely, it was the best of silk. 'Only if you tell me why you stared at me so this morning?'

'You can't be asking me that? You truly don't know?'

'Know what?' Sophie asked shaking her head. What was Phillippa saying?

'Pull off your gown, let's see if it fits. We aren't the same size, but I think in essentials, we're close.' Once Sophie stood there staring at herself in the mirror, Phillippa covered her mouth trying to hide a smile. 'You haven't thought of Mr Kittridge?'

'Thought of? He's a most entertaining man.'

'And that you are flirting with him?'

Sophie looked at the dress she wore. 'I thought you said no matchmaking. Is that what this gift is?'

'Truly, my dear, it no longer fits. But you . . . have not answered my question.'

Sophie's mouth opened in protest and then she closed it slowly. 'Do you wish me to ignore him while you are indisposed? Have him question your judgement at having such an ill-bred acquaintance?'

Phillippa smirked. 'That's all?'

'Well, as Lady Sandbourne even commented, he is fearful handsome.'

Absentmindedly Phillippa began to rearrange Sophie's hair to a more intricate style that fitted the dress. 'He's not a peer.'

Sophie watched her in the mirror of the dressing-table, an elaborate thing covered in tortoiseshell and brass that matched the room nicely. 'I'm still friends with you, aren't I?' Sophie teased, and heard an answering half-hidden chuckle.

Phillippa took a deep breath and leaned nearer Sophie's ear. 'Your Mr Kittridge discussed the sale with me. I'm not really sure why he's so interested in our house in London; compared to the house he's purchased in the country, it's a hovel.'

'He's not my anything.'

'Are you so sure?'

'I'm all but a pauper, in a family tainted with scandal. If he's looking for a wife, and his estate is so large, he'll need to find a girl of money and connections.'

'Who cares about a title or that he's in trade? In influence, he's a prince, Sophie.'

'Precisely the reason he might flirt with me to pass the time, but I should never expect anything more from the acquaintance. You told me you would not subject me to matchmaking. I'm already starting to wonder if the price of Lady Sandbourne's attentions isn't too high.'

'Oh, of course not, Sophie.' Phillippa paused as her smile grew. 'But if, perchance, you decided to pursue the acquaintance a little more, I would lend you all my support.'

Sophie erupted in laughter. 'How mercenary you are!'

The party broke up rather informally with the Beresfords not returning to London. Mr Kittridge had already left when Sophie came down for breakfast, leaving her to drive back to London alone. This time, however, she was flanked on both sides by the men that Mr Beresford had hired. One interrupted carriage ride was enough in his eyes.

Chapter Six

She arrived late in the evening and the entire house was lit up. Carriages lined up vying for a space to deposit their occupants; only the fact that she was being driven into the mews enabled her to get in at all.

'What's going on?' Sophie asked, as Inviolata met her.

'Miss Mariah's coming out. She was presented to the Queen this morning. It was supposed to be next week, but Lady Sandbourne persuaded some acquaintances and got her there early. A ball has just been announced for next week that she wants the two of you to attend. You'll need to get changed; Anjanette was told to help you.'

'Thank you, Inviolata.'

'Oh, Miss Greenwood, a gentleman dropped this by earlier for you.' The older woman handed over the letter. It was not signed or addressed, so there would be nothing for which anyone could reproach her.

I have hired some men for your protection. Any gentleman would do so to prevent another bruise marring such a fair neck.

Mr Kittridge never did anything just to be polite; he truly worried she might be attacked again. That certainly didn't make her feel any better.

Anjanette pulled out a gown Sophie hadn't seen before when they reached her room via the back stairs. It was a gauzy filmy thing of cream mull and covered with the most intricate silver embroidery.

'Did you have a pleasant stay?' Anjanette asked as she bustled about the room. For not coming as her maid, she was making a good show at performing the duties of one.

'For the most part; the man who attacked me appeared though. Only a closed gate saved me further injury. I hope the dress has long sleeves; he caught me by the arm.'

'I always knew Lady Sandbourne was a slave to fashion but this one, my goodness.' Anjanette's eyes grew round as she showed her a layer missing from one of the numerous underskirts which filled in the once very daring *décolletage* and allowed the tiny sleeves now to reach her wrists. Had Lady Sandbourne truly worn it open almost to the very waist?

'Phillippa gave me a dress of hers that no longer fits.'

'I'll look at it while you are at the ball then.'

'No, it fits perfectly and is the current fashion. You needn't do a thing to it.' Sitting before the mirror, Sophie looked up at Anjanette in the reflection. 'She didn't even include you at a function in her own house?'

Her silence was as telling as any words. Anjanette had Sophie's hair done both expertly and quickly, her head coiled extravagantly with a strand of pearls before Lady Sandbourne appeared at the door.

'Ah, there you are, child. I don't imagine you met anyone suitable while you were away. We'll have to make up the time lost now I suppose.' She clucked as if Sophie had been wasting her time. 'Go and find Mariah, please. Lady Elmhurst has been dying to see her dress.'

A week without being treated like a servant, or entertainment, went in an instant. Sophie's shoulders slumped with the fatigue of it all. And, of course, she found Mariah with Mr Fraser at the side door. He had not been invited.

'Don't tell my aunt, Sophie, please,' Mariah cried the moment she found them.

'Your reputation is her responsibility while we're in London under her care.'

'My reputation!' Mariah cried.

It really wasn't why Mariah thought Sophie brought up such things, but reputation was all they had. If Lady Sandbourne even suspected such a thing, Mariah would be sitting with some man she'd never care a whit about while the one she truly thought she was in love with was run off for good. 'Go and find your aunt; she wants to show off your dress.'

'But —' Mariah complained.

'We'll go riding in the morning; getting caught now won't do either of you any good. The servants are everywhere; if just one sees you, Lady Sandbourne will make sure it never happens again.'

Mr Fraser didn't need any more argument than that. He vanished into the night.

'Sophie, how can I thank you.'

'Just go and keep your aunt happy.' Once Mariah was back in sight of the guests, there wasn't a word said to Sophie. She'd had a tiring journey back to London and no one cared that she was back. She climbed two steps up the staircase to slip away —

'Sophie, child.'

She'd recognize Mr Dyson's voice anywhere. At least there was one friendly face to be seen. As Sophie turned, she recognized Mr Kittridge at his side, too.

'Why didn't you tell me of these dreadful attacks as soon as they happened?'

'I rather thought Mr Kittridge would have mentioned it at the opera the other evening. He was the one who saved me the first time.'

Mr Dyson shook his head and turned to Mr Kittridge. 'You knew all that time and I had to hear about it from the gossips?'

Mr Kittridge smiled faintly, his blue eyes sparkling with more humour than he let his countenance show. 'I didn't realize Miss Greenwood knew everyone in London.'

'She doesn't, she knows me! Since she was but a scrawny child.'

'I think I might ask for this dance, Miss Greenwood, before Mr Dyson starts making a scene,' Mr Kittridge interrupted. 'If it isn't already taken?'

'No,' Sophie murmured, and before Mr Dyson could say anything else, Mr Kittridge had her whisked away to the dancing. 'You could have just told me of the men guarding me instead of leaving a note anyone could have seen,' she whispered, as she took her place in the line of dancers.

'I might have, had I known I was coming this evening.'

'You weren't invited?'

'I seem to remember telling you I was going to avoid balls. Dyson and I both came as guests of another. I thought I was meeting him as a matter of business, actually.'

'Ever the hard worker, aren't you? Everywhere I go it seems you are there for business.'

He smiled down at her as they came together. 'It saves me from mothers throwing their daughters at me wherever I go. I work far less then you imagine.'

He was the only man who had danced with her since she came to London and he, of course, only to be polite. 'Heavens, you seem to positively dislike the idea of women altogether.' It was more to tease, there was little other way to make the most of the few dances she would have this season.

'Not at all, just mothers throwing their marriageable daughters at me.'

No, she couldn't be so unwarrantably presumptious, could she? but she just couldn't hold her tongue. 'Are you worth catching then, Mr Kittridge, if they think so highly of you?'

He was unable to respond immediately as they were separated as others made their way past. For several moments as they made the figures of the dance, he just gave her a puzzled look.

'Do you always spar with words, Miss Greenwood?' Mr Kittridge asked eventually as they came together again.

'Would you prefer I flattered you on the skill of your steps, or the cut of your suit? I can do either well, but I rather thought we were past trivial conversations.'

'I was confirming not criticizing, Miss Greenwood.'

Even though they were close enough to speak, for some time Sophie remained silent. She had sounded like her mother did with her father. There was wit and there was being a shrew. 'I suppose I have the opposite history of having people thrown at me. If I sound bitter, do forgive me.'

The music ended abruptly as Roberts made the announcement presenting Mariah for her first dance. Just she and the four other girls who had been presented at Court that day took their places before everyone, with — knowing Lady Sandbourne — the highest-ranking gentlemen there.

'I should imagine you made a fairer picture at your presentation.' Mr Kittridge whispered in her ear.

Looking over her shoulder, she was relieved to see that he was further away than she thought, certainly not close enough to cause gossip. 'Idle flattery, Mr Kittridge, it's a time I try to forget.' Sophie replied without thinking. She looked back again quickly. 'I'm doing it again, aren't I? My provenance really isn't that of harpy.'

His chuckle glided over her like a song as much as his voice did. 'I'm sure if you find a suitable man to flatter you on a regular basis all those sharp words would not find time to slip out.'

Sophie started laughing at how much of a farcical thought that was. His was the longest conversation she had been allowed since she came to London. Her retort died in her throat though when she caught sight of Lady Sandbourne across the room.

'Miss Greenwood, if you would permit me, I've supper and cards with some acquaintances on Wednesday evening. You would be most welcome to join us. It would, regrettably, keep you away from the house while your cousin is at Almack's.'

'In that case, I would be delighted.'

'I'll ask Miss Asquith and her brother to call at seven then.' Mr Kittridge waved to Lady Sandbourne standing at the door before he walked off. Sophie bit her lip to keep from smiling at Lady Sandbourne's disapproving stare. How did he know she was keeping watch? Was it any wonder none ever dared speak to her?

She had barely finished breakfast after their ride in the park to meet Mr Fraser, when Lady Sandbourne insisted Sophie change into a pale peach dress covered with ivory lace, one of the finest that Sophie had been presented with. Why she was so insistent was anyone's guess. Fortunately, it too, had long sleeves so the bruises that covered her arm where the man had grabbed her the second time were hidden.

'Where are we going?' Sophie asked finally.

'We have someone to meet,' was the only answer she received.

It was a fine day, and the top was down on the barouche giving Sophie a good view of all around her. Her gaze always seemed to scan the crowd looking for an unkempt blond haired man. He seemed nowhere in view, but several times Sophie caught sight of the men who could only be those guarding her. She hadn't set eyes on them before, but one muscular fellow tipped his hat at her notice as she looked at him for perhaps the fifth time.

They were soon admitted to a residence a few streets away. The room they were shown into was filled with magnificent carved mahogany furniture upholstered with gold silk brocade. Sophie's heart leapt to her chest for a moment when she saw a man at the window as they were introduced to the elderly lady.

'Lady Graemoor, how kind of you to see us. I know you don't receive many visitors,' Lady Sandbourne announced.

They all curtsied, but before Sophie could even stand upright, Lady Sandbourne was pushing her toward the older lady.

'What a pretty child you've brought with you, too,' Lady Graemoor announced, a little too loudly. Her gentle hand patted the seat next to her as the man turned finally and Sophie blanched. It wasn't just her imagination. She hadn't learned the man's name, but she wouldn't forget the look on his elegant, weasel-like face when he had turned from her on hearing the news of her family two years earlier. This visit was set up for them to meet, only he was the last man she ever wished to see again. And she was certain she was the last woman he would willingly marry. He had made that sentiment quite clear two years before.

'Are you well, Sophie? You look as if you are ready to faint.' Mariah asked, loud enough for the man to come forward to steady her.

'No, I am well,' she said, before he could assist her. He bowed to her forcing her to acknowledge him with one of her own. He smiled at her; he didn't even remember who she was.

'Who do you have with you today, Lady Sandbourne?' Lady Graemoor asked, as Sophie took a step away from him. Old, no, the woman seemed positively ancient as she neared Lady Graemoor.

'My niece, Miss Mariah Randolph, and her cousin, the Honorable Miss Sophie Greenwood.'

Sophie watched him, saw the recognition of the name at least wash across his face. His smile remained but the easiness she had seen a moment before vanished.

'I've heard that name before, haven't I?' Lady Graemoor asked gently.

Lady Sandbourne smiled faintly. 'She was attacked brutally just outside my door only a few weeks ago. Everyone seems to have heard her name.'

'Poor child. You must stay for supper and tell me all about it.'

How could she let the charade continue? The grandson would inform her soon enough of the rest of her past. 'Another evening perhaps?' Sophie rushed to say before Lady Sandbourne could answer. Lady Sandbourne's eyes narrowed and Sophie knew they had been there for her, not Mariah.

'Tomorrow then. I'm sure my evening will be absolutely dull with everyone dashing about now that people have returned to Town for the season,' Lady Graemoor offered.

Sophie kept her mouth shut not wanting to provoke Lady Sandbourne's displeasure. No one answered though.

'Well, are you free, girl?'

'Tomorrow I have no engagements, Lady Graemoor.'

'Good. And what about every week.'

'What?' *Well, as there was no chance to not cause more displeasure, she might as well get it over with,* Sophie thought.

Lady Graemoor laughed gently, but Sophie kept her eyes on her grandson. He wouldn't even look at her; he kept his gaze firmly on Lady Sandbourne. 'Now, how are you ever to find a husband if you turn down invitations?' Well, that got his attention. His head flew around to stare at his grandmother.

'Grandmother, no,' Lord Graemoor ejaculated a little too loudly. Both of the older women turned to him, staring at his unexpected words.

Enough. Sophie took a deep breath. 'I'll find a husband the same way your grandson wishes to find a wife: by turning my back on someone because a father lost a girl's dowry through misfortune, and a mother who tried to marry her off before anyone knew.' Lady Graemoor stared at her, but even with Lady Sandbourne's annoyed gaze, Sophie could not stop. 'The girl knew nothing of her parents' actions until she watched your grandson turn his back on her with only one word — pity.' He tore at my heart that night, and we'd never even spoken a word. Now, I won't let myself be sold on false pretences to a man who would resent me so blatantly for the rest of my days should you two exert your influence.'

With that, Sophie walked out. She didn't stop at the front door, or even the carriage. She just walked down the street without a chaperon. She had walked the length of the street when a shout caught her attention. Spinning around, she saw it was only a street vendor, but her eyes flitted around as she realized she had placed herself without the protection of even a boy to call for help. And she'd claimed she had Jasper's share of sense. Both shares had obviously left her in her anger.

A carriage slowed as it neared her, her carriage, the barouche she brought in trade for dresses. No one was inside, but at least the driver was there. Sophie felt rather than saw the presence of the men she remembered were her guards. Her heart slowed gradually. Why had she returned to London? She had known it would be like this.

Barely over the sting of Earl Graemoor and the look he gave at the mention of marriage, Lady Sandbourne told Sophie to dress especially carefully for dinner that night. Wearing the gown Phillippa had given her, she felt beautiful as they left the house. Their hostess, a Mrs Meade, presented Sophie to Lord Dunalan her dinner companion before leading them to the silk-draped dining-room. Lady Sandbourne smiled at the pair before she left them to be seated. There was an entire turkey gracing the middle of the table.

'Here, let me serve you some curry of rabbit?' he asked, before she'd even had a chance to remove her napkin from her blue and white plate.

'No, thank you, I'd rather have the buttered lobster.' She indicated that he pass it her way.

'Oh, then, sweetbreads?' Lord Dunahan

asked, passing a new plate in her direction.

'No, I'd prefer some of the macaroni.'

'Some vegetable pudding?'

'No, thank you, I would prefer the peach fritters.'

They hadn't even reached the second course, their only conversation him trying to hand her dishes she did not want. Then he leaned over.

'Miss Greenwood, I have an offer for you. . . .' The next words were whispered.

Sophie could only be glad no one else had heard such language. Scandal-ridden her name might be, she could hardly credit being spoken to like a common harlot.

'Sir! You will remove yourself from my company. I demand it.'

'Come now . . . you'll find no better offer and you are a handsome woman. It would be a shame for you to end an old maid.'

Sophie slowly drank her wine trying to reconcile the fact that he thought her low enough to consider such a base offer after knowing her all of perhaps twenty minutes. It made her anger rise to the occasion. 'I have men standing guard outside. If you insist in pursuing even conversation with me, they will deal with you the moment you step out of the door.'

He closed his mouth slowly. Sophie went

back to her food, hiding a smile when he excused himself from the table. After dinner, Countess Rossington asked about the attack, but otherwise hardly said a word to her. Lord Southworth all but made love to her in the presence of the entire room as they gathered for coffee, but Lady Sandbourne whisked her away when it was obvious he wasn't looking for a bride. A Mr Hewlett tried to speak to her, but lost his nerve when Lady Sandbourne and another widow flanked her, the only reason she could gather why, was the hushed whisper *trade.*

Sophie closed the door behind her ready to scream, as Mariah kept talking about the wonderful dinner. That she kept her mouth closed to muffle the sound of her frustration, she considered the height of restraint.

'Are you well, Miss Greenwood?' Anjanette asked.

Only then did Sophie open her eyes to find Anjanette working on yet another dress. 'A man offered me *carte blanche,* a man I had never met until this very night. All because my father is imprudent and my mother ridiculous.'

The dress fell from Anjanette's hand in surprise. 'I confess I am amazed he truly asked such a thing? You're certain?'

'Indeed, there could be little doubt from his words. I've not heard such vulgar language in all my life. Such manners and from a peer no less.'

For a moment Anjanette made no remark.

'You certainly don't think I should have taken his offer?' Sophie gasped.

'Oh dear me no, don't think that of my silence.' Anjanette laid the dress in her lap before staring out of the window.

'Anjanette, what is the matter?'

The corner of Anjanette's mouth turned down in a look of complete contempt. 'Matter? I've had such an offer myself. I suppose the shock never goes.'

Sophie couldn't help but remember her words. Her mother thought her not a good connection and she had not left Kent until now. 'My . . . Jasper surely didn't make such — ?'

Anjanette didn't let her finish the sentence. 'No, your brother is indeed the finest gentleman I know. Your mother came with the offer when she heard Jasper might propose marriage. She could not see me as the next Lady Canmore.'

'Jasper might be without sense time and again, but he would not countenance that decision.'

Anjanette's hand curled around the arm of the chair in silence. 'It all happened just days before you were brought home from London. Jasper couldn't support any wife after your mother's behaviour. I've only a few thousand pounds, not enough, Jasper said. I should save it for a man who could support me. You weren't the only one hurt when that ship went down.'

'I wondered why Papa wanted you to see London,' Sophie whispered, more to herself than out loud.

'And now you know why your mother sent word it was to be as your maid.'

Mama, oh what a mess you have created. Now she was the connection no one wished to have; Mama had become her own nightmare. Wait, *Dearest*. Jasper called her *Dearest* in the letter; he never called Sophie that. The letter wasn't for her it was for Anjanette. Papa had misunderstood. 'Anjanette, do you know anyone named Greyfriars?'

'Greyfriars.' Anjanette sat there for so long Sophie wondered if perhaps she might not get an answer. 'Why would you ask such a question?'

Sophie went to her trunk and pulled the letter from the lining where she had hidden it. 'I believe this was meant for you.'

Tears fell down Anjanette's cheek as she

read it. 'I might have been the one attacked if not for your papa's mistake.'

'Everyone's mistake, whoever the man is, he saw a letter Jasper sent to Papa and jumped to the same conclusion. He said so when he had his hands around my throat. He saw the letter.'

'Jasper's sense does seem to have gone awry in this instance. I don't know who Greyfriars is either, even if the letter was meant for me.'

Sophie sank into a chair overwhelmed, a stranger still stalked her, the outcome of which was in doubt. It was indeed a case of mistaken identity after all, but for the attention to be thrown on a friend certainly wasn't a fine solution to the matter.

Sophie brushed out her hair preparing for bed when a faint knock sounded.

'Come.' She was surprised to find it was Lady Sandbourne in a wrapper herself, also ready for bed.

'I didn't know Lady Graemoor would push a match so soon. She has been trying to marry off her grandson for years. I thought you might have much in common.'

'I didn't know his name to be able to say I would not be agreeable to such a match.'

'I was here more to speak to you about

109

Mr Kittridge. You shouldn't be so free with your favours,' she replied. 'Trade isn't suitable for a woman of your standing.'

The marchioness had condescended to have her company and she had obviously decided it was up to her as to who was worthy even to speak to Sophie. Mr Fraser too; Mariah was obviously too good for him. Sophie just couldn't listen to it anymore. 'Heaven forbid. Do you forget where you were born? If not for your father's money, no marquess would have looked at you. My father wouldn't care if I married a shopkeeper in York as long as I had an affection at marriage. There are things more important than a title.

'I should like to know why you are bringing him up at all. He was a guest of the Beresfords at Easter. I cannot escape the acquaintance even if I wished to. He saved my life. While you spend your days gossiping about the incident, he's hired men to protect me. My attacker has been to Coverly Court.'

Lady Sandbourne turned red at Sophie's bringing up her background. 'Sophie —'

'No, I cannot allow you to dictate to whom I may speak or dance. I had one dance with him and you imply I'm throwing myself at him shamelessly at every turn.

My conduct was never brought in to question and I have not been a flirt, trying to catch the eye of any man who crosses my path. But while we're on that matter, I wonder if I shall encounter Mr Fraser again.'

'What does Mr Fraser have to do with you?' Lady Sandbourne's words were harsh.

Sophie spun around; it was as much of a confession as she would ever receive that Lady Sandbourne had been keeping him from Mariah. 'He's a most agreeable, amiable man. You were right; I shouldn't have dismissed him and his estate in Scotland. It was wrong of me and I should like to know him better.'

'Sophie, what do you think you are about?'

'I said my coming to London was an escape from home. I would like to have conversation while I am here, but none of your acquaintances will condescend to speak to me. I am tired of it. The rout this evening was only one of many times I said not a word to another besides Mariah. Mr Fraser was the only one to ask me to dance at the ball, since when you've introduced Mariah to many eligible men. Mr Kittridge was the only man who danced with me the evening of Mariah's presentation.'

'I have someone in mind for you, Sophie. He's not come up from the country yet.'

'In addition to the ten I've already met? I think I would prefer to speak to my mother than wait for a *carte-blanche* from those men for whom you've singled me out.'

Lady Sandbourne paled as Sophie took her leave and left the bedroom. Obviously the men had not hinted at the offers they had in mind when she had been selling Sophie's charms.

Sophie eventually found solitude in a far corner of the house in a decorated room in the French style that was little used. A maid followed behind like a shadow and lit the fire for her while a glass of ratafia appeared in her hand.

Unable to bear the thought of returning home so soon, Sophie's only worry was whether she could endure the rest of the summer in Lady Sandbourne's home. Was there truly only the prospect of becoming a man's mistress? Five of the men she had met had been living on a few hundred pounds a year. She didn't ask for much in a man, but even such a match seemed impossible when Lady Sandbourne discouraged anyone not up to her standards.

In her line of sight was an old shield, far older than most of the furnishings in the room. The Marquess of Sandbourne's coat of arms was painted on it, one of those convoluted things with quartering, and crosshatching and who knew what else. Sophie sat up straight in her chair when she saw the bearers on the side. Greyfriars! Was it a bearer for the man's arms? Was it part of the man's arms itself? Had Jasper known he was being watched as he wrote the letters and given a clue to the man's name? Sophie rushed quickly to the bell and rang for Roberts.

The wait was interminable, but eventually he appeared. 'Roberts, I think you might know the answer to a question I have: do you know of any family which has Greyfriars attached to their arms in any way?'

He said nothing about her having called him so late in the evening, or that she was in her nightclothes. His brow knitted in thought for some time. 'I'm sorry to say I don't think there is, miss.'

Her heart fell. 'Not as bearers even?'

'I've seen fishermen, mermaids, animals but no friars.'

'Thank you, Roberts.' Sophie had been so certain. Of course, Jasper had been sure the name would mean something as well and he had been wrong; another case of his sense being a little lacking.

She went back to her bed but the puzzle kept her from sleeping, so she turned her mind to more agreeable thoughts. She would never admit to anyone that she occupied her mind with Mr Kittridge.

CHAPTER SEVEN

Mr Fraser had to be away from London for several days leaving Sophie to ride in the park alone while Mariah slept late once again. They hardly spoke now, the longer they were in London the more it became apparent they were separate guests: separate visits, separate calls. Sophie hadn't gone out with Mariah for over a week and with Mr Fraser away, even their morning rides were curtailed.

'Your carriage is here to take you for dinner,' Mariah announced, upon entering Sophie's room as she dressed for dinner. 'You aren't dressed yet? The Pomona green gown would complement your hairstyle. Why not wear it tonight? I do love those roses you embroidered at the hem.'

Not even considering another, Sophie dressed quickly so she wouldn't keep Miss Asquith waiting.

'I hope you enjoy yourself.'

'I'm sure I shall.'

'I do miss you being with us at Almack's. My aunt is quite persistent in introducing me to some duke or other who cares nothing for me and who seldom speaks.'

Almost out of the door, Sophie stopped at the sight of Mariah who looked very pretty and very young. 'Mariah, don't let your aunt dissuade you if you really like Mr Fraser.'

Mariah laughed slightly. 'Have I ever been dissuaded from anything?'

'Then you have decided on him for certain?'

'He has not asked yet, Sophie.' Her cousin's smiling eyes laughed even if she did not. 'But I think his is the only offer I should accept if I should receive one.'

'Even though he doesn't have a title?'

'Now you sound like Aunt Sandbourne. Papa introduced me to Mr Fraser. He desires the connections of Lady Naismith's brother, Mr Fraser's father. Therefore, you see, I would be fulfilling my father's wishes as well as my own feelings. Go, you have an engagement.'

Miss Asquith looked as if she was sucking on a lemon as she and her brother walked Sophie to their carriage.

'Miss Greenwood, I was most happy to hear we'd have another lady for our evening.

There were too many men tonight so it worked out splendidly when Mr Kittridge proposed you.' The Asquiths were rather a study in family resemblance. Each had the same shade of brown hair, the same shade of brown eyes, and each was just slightly chubby.

Mr Asquith talked all through the ride. He wasn't overbearing, just kept up amiable conversation while his sister, Charlotte, said not a word.

On being shown inside the house, which was modest by Mayfair standards, it was apparent why Miss Asquith had a problem. There was a married couple, several more Asquith brothers and Mr Kittridge. Until the day before, Miss Asquith would have been the only single woman. Sophie was competition and, as the other single men were Charlotte's siblings, her cap must have been set at Mr Kittridge.

'Ah, Miss Greenwood,' Mr Kittridge said, when he saw her. 'You must be introduced. Our hosts Sir George Steedmond and his wife, Lady Steedmond, Mr and Mrs Godfrey, and, of course, the Asquiths, Mr Nicholas Asquith, and his sons, Mr Simon and Mr Matthew. You met Mr Charles and Miss Charlotte on the drive here.'

If Charles and Charlotte were two peas in

a pod, then the entire family sat in there with them as all were of similar height, weight, and colouring. The Godfreys were a study in opposites, one fair, the other dark, one slim, the other heavy, one tall the other short. That left Sir George and Lady Steedmond. She was a widowed countess now married to her baronet husband; it was in their house where the party was taking place, Charles Asquith had informed her on the way there.

Mr Kittridge held out his arm for her to take when supper was announced moments later.

'I don't think Miss Asquith is happy,' Sophie whispered, as she caught sight of the table — salmon, ham, chicken, rabbit, veal, venison, goose, lobster, and she hadn't even a good look at the side dishes yet.

'She was was living in Cornwall until this week and was presented at Court recently. She's not been out before. I'm not sure she knows how to even speak in public.'

'You mistook me, Mr Kittridge. I think she sees me as competition for your attentions.'

'Aren't you?'

Sophie tried very hard not to blush while enduring Miss Asquith glaring at her from across the table when she was seated next to Mr Kittridge.

'Have you heard from the Beresfords? I do hope Mrs Beresford is over her illness,' Mr Kittridge asked, as the footman passed the dish of peas and potatoes.

'They didn't tell you? She's expecting their first child.'

Mr Kittridge laughed slightly. 'No wonder.'

'Miss Greenwood.' Sophie turned her head to the new voice. 'I believe I heard you are staying with the Marchioness of Sandbourne?' Lady Steedmond asked.

'Yes, my lady. She is my cousin's aunt.'

'I see she is still trying to marry girls off every season then.'

'I thought that was just my impression.'

Lady Steedmond laughed heartily. 'Oh, no, dear, ever since the marquess died, she has had a girl or two to stay with her. I believe she has seen all of them married before the end of the season.'

'I fear she may fail with me then if her attempts so far are any indication.'

'Lady Sandbourne admit defeat? Never,' Sir George added.

'My lady, you've a fine chaise. Is it new?' Miss Asquith asked, taking the lady's attention from Sophie.

'Not one man interested? I find that hard

to believe.' Mr Kittridge spoke just loud enough for her to hear, his lilting voice taking away the formality of the evening.

She knew it was unwarrantably bold to speak of such things, but she just couldn't hold her tongue. 'For marriage? No, not one.'

His eyebrow rose as he took a sip of his turtle soup. 'I hope you sent them on their way.'

'I threatened one with harm from the men you hired.' Sophie loved to hear his laughter fill the room.

'What is so funny, Mr Kittridge?' the elder Mr Asquith asked.

'An interesting comment concerning a mutual acquaintance. I fear you would find it tedious,' he announced, to hide the real reason. He turned to her again. 'You've had no trouble since they were hired?'

'I should not have let you do it. If anyone finds out, they might think there is an attachment where none is meant.'

He turned his head and staring right at her, his voice lowered. 'Miss Greenwood, do you think I go around complimenting all the women I meet as I do you, dangling after them?'

'I. . . .' It was the most she could get out and it made his grin grow.

'Is the food too spicy, Miss Greenwood?' Sir George asked.

Mr Kittridge handed Sophie her glass. 'Miss Greenwood swallowed badly, I think. The meal is most excellent,' he lied.

'After what you know?' Sophie asked under her breath.

'What do I know? Your father tried to improve his fortune and was unfortunate in the weather. Your mother, while imprudent, saved me wishing you not married to some man who was only after your twenty thousand pounds.'

'We've only known each other for a few weeks yet you make such statements? You forget my brother's indiscretions too?'

'You wish me to show interest in Miss Asquith, who won't say a word to me, or a hundred like her? I didn't come to find a wife, but I have found a friend in you, Miss Greenwood —'

'What are you speaking of so intently?' Miss Asquith asked, the first words Sophie had heard spoken directly to her.

'Miss Greenwood was asking if my brother should like to meet you, Miss Asquith. He'll be coming to England in the next year or so and as I am likely to be far too busy to show him London properly, she thought you might do an admirable job of it.'

'Does he resemble you much? Fine manners, correct opinions?'

'In those instances yes; many say he is the more handsome though.'

The young woman's eyes lit up at the idea, then Mr Godfrey started talking to Sophie and the topic came to an end.

After two full courses and dessert, two tables of cards were set up. Not everyone could play since they were an odd number for a third. Sophie had been reading at a quaint lady's painted writing desk for about ten minutes when she sensed Mr Kittridge sit nearby, actually smelled the bay rum still in his clothes. She glanced around, but no one else was at the end of the room near them.

'You would call me friend?' she whispered almost afraid to voice it out loud. There had been so few she had met as new acquaintances who did not disdain her for her family's behaviour. She did not expect to hear such words.

'Many have tried to make my acquaintance since I arrived in London, very few have not done so for their own benefit. Even my hosts tonight wish me to put money into a venture. The Beresfords and you are about the only people who have not forced more upon me than friendship. And, of you, I should like to know far more.'

Sophie looked at him from the corner of her eye. 'I take it there is still more about you than I know.'

His laugh was quiet, not attracting the others in the room. 'Then I know why Lady Sandbourne holds me in such disregard. Am I so new to Town that no one has heard a thing about me to temper the stigma of trade?'

Sophie lifted her head from her book, closing it slowly. She couldn't help herself. 'Even if you weren't in trade, you would have the title of mushroom to be used against you.'

'Perhaps, but how many — ?'

'Miss Greenwood,' Lady Steedmond called from her cards. 'I hear from Mr Asquith that Mr Kittridge says you play divinely. Perhaps you would entertain us with some music? Haydn has always been a favourite of mine and so few play well.'

'Go, play, for I haven't exaggerated your skill,' Mr Kittridge offered.

'How many what?'

The smile filled his eyes when he looked up as she stood. 'How many can claim pirates as their forebears, so how can I be called a mushroom? The money is not so very new, just not quite so very legal. Gentry in England or Jamaica, either way we've been at it for some time. The pirates were a long way back.'

'Come, Miss Greenwood, please.'

Sophie tried not to laugh as Sonata in C started to fill the room. That had to be the first time long-ago theft had been used as an argument against being new money.

The evening broke up near midnight. Several of the guests were riding back in a single carriage, at least until Mr Nicholas Asquith asked to be dropped at Crockford's, the gaming hell, and his brother followed him out.

Sophie stared across at Mr Kittridge. 'You don't join them?'

'And have you address me in a stern tone if I should lose my fortune on a gamble? I think not.' Miss Asquith gasped at such words and little more was said as they continued the drive home. Miss Asquith's other brother tried not to laugh.

'You promised you would dance with me at the Pattersons' ball, Mr Kittridge. You won't forget?' Miss Asquith asked, when the silence became too stifling.

'I said the next ball I attended, I'm afraid, and I'm engaged the evening of the Pattersons' ball. I was planning to attend the Chancellors' ball if you want to hold me to my promise.'

This time when the silence returned it wasn't broken again, at least not before they reached Lady Sandbourne's.

'Will you be attending the Chancellors' ball?' Mr Asquith asked, as Sophie made to leave the carriage — frankly Sophie couldn't remember which brother was which: they all looked so much alike.

'I believe so.'

'Good, then I'll ask the first dance of you now before the rush starts. Kittridge, do claim one. It would do you ill to promise my sister and leave our other fair guest without the same.'

He said nothing at first, but then, giving her his hand in help down, whispered, 'I'll ask for all that are not claimed by others, Miss Greenwood. But Miss Asquith doesn't need to hear that. If you would allow me, I could make enquiries so you might determine your brother's condition and perhaps learn your attacker's identity, at the very least.'

It was too much. He knew all yet wished to help her in spite of it. 'Is that possible? The army is so large, I wouldn't even know where to start.'

'Do you forget I supply the Royal Navy with rum? I know men enough; it should be no great task. His details and your permission to act on your behalf are all I need.'

Could she go through the summer just waiting? 'After you saved my life, I owe you enough already,' she whispered. As much as she wanted to know, how could she become more indebted to him? Still, to put an end to all this mess. . . . 'Ensign Jasper Greenwood, 77th Regiment of Foot. As his letter said, he's with Picton in the Peninsular Campaign. But, with Paris surrounded, I don't quite know where he is now,' she announced. 'Thank you, Mr Kittridge.' Only then did he let go of her hand. As Sophie walked into the house, she remembered telling him she hardly danced at any of the balls she attended. He had all but claimed every one.

CHAPTER EIGHT

The Chancellors' ball came quickly. Late that afternoon, Mariah rushed about not for a ballgown but for a gown to wear at supper. Mr Fraser was coming to dine. Mariah looked flustered, falling against the door after she came in.

'I just received a letter from Papa,' she blurted out. 'He says Mr Fraser was there asking permission for my hand and Papa gave it.'

'But your aunt will never leave you alone with him for just that reason.'

'He can take his time, Sophie. I know he intends to and that is all that really matters.' Then her face sobered. 'Oh, I suppose I should tell you there is another for dinner tonight as well. Viscount Hodgkin has just come up from the country.'

Sophie had a sinking feeling that he was the one Lady Sandbourne had in mind for her. 'Do you know anything about him?'

'I think I heard his granddaughter is coming with him. She was presented at Court recently.'

'He's as old as my grandpapa?'

'Why, does it matter?'

'Your aunt said she was waiting for someone she had in mind for me to come from the country.'

Mariah's mouth formed an O. 'She can't think you'd be a match. She can't think your father would approve a union with a man who has a daughter as old as your mother.'

'I don't know what she thinks anymore.'

The knock on the door made them both start. 'Your guests are arriving,' the maid announced.

'Who is it, Suzanna?'

'Mr Fraser; Lady Sandbourne isn't dressed yet.'

'Go quickly. I'll help her finish and you can speak alone,' Sophie suggested.

'I don't know that he's going to ask.'

'Well he surely won't if Lady Sandbourne is there and he'll have wasted his time going to see your father.'

'Excellent point.' Mariah rushed off.

Sophie went to Lady Sandbourne's room down the hall and knocked. 'Do you need any help?'

'You are a good girl, Sophie. You don't deserve the situation you are in. Yes, if you could bring me my amethyst set, it should go well with the dress, once Mrs Woods finishes pressing it at any rate. It came from the mantua-maker badly wrinkled. Inviolata has been so busy with you and Mariah that I found I had nothing new to wear myself.'

'You've a closetful of gowns you haven't worn more than once.'

'Precisely.'

Nearly twenty minutes later, they found their way downstairs. Mariah and Mr Fraser were sitting opposite each other at a table playing cards while the maid served them wine. No one else had yet arrived.

Lady Sandbourne all but sniffed her displeasure. 'I hadn't heard you had arrived already, Mr Fraser,' she said cordially enough, but the two cousins hadn't missed a thing.

The moment Lady Sandbourne turned her back, Mariah started grinning and nodded quickly. *So they were engaged.* Would it be a long engagement, she wondered, for Lady Sandbourne would surely not make Sophie welcome without her cousin to entertain? She had promised them marriage by summer's end, but Lady Sandbourne had had nothing to do with Mr Fraser. He was too far beneath Mariah in the marchioness's opinion. Was it that, or was it that Lady Sandbourne wasn't in control and she demanded it?

'Viscount Hodgkin, his granddaughter Miss Augustine Bellingham, and Viscount Wolfenway and his sister, Miss Caroline Wolfenway, may I present my niece, Miss Mariah Randolph, and her cousin, Miss Sophie Greenwood,' Lady Sandbourne announced. *Now, who was for her?*

'My pleasure, I'm sure.' Viscount Wolfenway bowed deeply. Both he and his sister were painted peacocks but neither had beauty enough to draw the eye without their grand attire. 'I shall have to invite you to my home in the country. Wolfenhame End is the most beautiful house in Wales, if I do say so myself.' The moment he stood, Sophie felt as if she was a cow on display for a buyer. His eyes never left her, and not in a good way. It wasn't true interest, it was judgement. Inside, Sophie screamed while she remained outwardly calm, as Lady Sandbourne led them in to dinner. Sophie hadn't noticed that other guests had arrived until she was seated next to a man whom she had not met before. The dinner was far less grand than the one earlier that week,

130

only oyster sauce, fish, fowls, and beef for the first course. Lady Sandbourne was surely not in the mood to impress anyone.

'Mr Bowlins, miss. I think our hostess is a little preoccupied tonight.' Sophie looked around and found the viscount nowhere near her at the table. He was seated next to Mariah and giving her the same look Sophie had just experienced. Lady Sandbourne looked smug as Mr Fraser had to sit next to the dull sister, Caroline, at the other end of the table.

Sophie slowly turned to Lady Sandbourne who seemed to be waiting for her gaze. The smug look of satisfaction was answer enough.

Only at the ball, after dinner, was Sophie even close to being alone with Mariah. Before she was hardly through the door, Mr Asquith, who had claimed a dance, was at her side.

'Miss Greenwood, would you grant me the first two dances.'

'Of course.' It's not as if anyone else would claim them; they were intriguing words from Mr Kittridge, but she didn't really expect him to endure criticism by dancing all the dances with her alone.

'I hear they're going to dance a waltz this

evening,' Mr Asquith said, as they waited for the music to start.

'Really?'

'Almack's allowed the first one to be danced there last week. Miss Chancellor wishes to show off her skill at learning it.'

Even worse, Viscount Wolfenway stared across at both of them as they waited. The music started and they began the figures, but Sophie had gone cold inside. Mr Asquith didn't even speak as if she might have been at Almack's, but had just thrown it in her face that he knew she wasn't. He tried saying several things after that, but Sophie didn't hear them. Nothing was worth the price of being away from her mother. She knew then what was coming. In London, people she hardly knew insulted her. How did one prepare when it could come from anyone? The same as the attacks on her: how could she prevent them when the man could jump out at any moment? She was a prisoner.

'It was me, Sophie, me she's trying to sell off,' Mariah hissed, when she got close enough. 'Papa might have given his permission, but she'll never let us have any peace and give hers.'

'You don't need it. Your Papa's permission is all that matters.'

It was their turn to move through the line of people, in and out, until they were standing next to each other again.

'Sophie, what are you saying?'

'Find Mr Fraser and decide a date. Send word to your parents to make the preparations and say you'll be there. Go and spend your honeymoon in that Glensheen he inherited. We can enjoy the season for a while longer.'

'I don't think I can do it, the viscount's been staring at me for so long.'

Sophie took a quick look to where he stood, still staring. 'Very good point. Well then, the barouche is sitting at the house, take it, and see it done. I'll bear your aunt's displeasure alone.'

If it weren't their turn to move again, Mariah would have frozen in her spot. Again, she had to wait to answer.

'I had forgotten about you. You would have to return home, wouldn't you? Even worse, explain to your mother why you returned early.'

'Phillippa has invited me to Coverly after the season is over. I could visit her for a time and put off home.'

'I can't ruin your summer, it's only May. I shall plan it at season's end and you can be a bridesmaid,' Mariah whispered.

With a final run through the procession of people, the musician signalled the end and they were able to escape to the supper room. 'What about the viscount?'

'I take it you don't want him either?'

Sophie shuddered. 'Heaven forbid.'

Mariah started to laugh. 'Then we can run him off with our shocking behaviour. I'll endure a little criticism if I can effect that.'

Sophie's lack of conversation with him at last seemed to offend Mr Asquith and, as the second dance ended, he rushed off to find a more amiable partner. She caught sight of Mr Kittridge standing up with Miss Asquith for the second two dances. A man was looking at her, but an older woman was speaking in his ear. His eyes went wide and he turned away quickly. Sophie took her cup of punch outside. A smallish garden was tucked behind the house and she sank onto the bench with a sigh. Fully enclosed on all sides there was no chance her attacker might find her, no chance anyone inside would see her in her humiliation. Lady Sandbourne with all her connections couldn't persuade a man to dance with her; her hopes of finding her a husband were certainly slim.

'So, do you waltz, Miss Greenwood?'

Sophie just about jumped out of her skin. It could have been anyone; more to the point, it could have been her attacker — she never heard a sound. It was Mr Kittridge though, the musical tones of his voice were all she needed to hear to let her know who had discovered her hiding place. 'It is certainly not a skill you learn from a country governess. Mama will still be quoting some book that calls it scandalous when my young sisters are finally old enough for their seasons.'

'Should you like to learn? I don't see your mother here to object.'

Sophie turned quickly only to find Mr Kittridge far nearer than she realized. His piercing blue eyes bore into her and a tiny bit of her wished it was for her sake. She wasn't vain, but still, to imagine someone might consider . . . if only not for her mother and brother. But who would seriously consider such a connection?

'You needn't offer just to be polite.'

'I'm sure they'd use much more colourful language to get the point across' — Mr Kittridge held his hand out for her to take — 'but there's a shipful of men I sailed here with who will inform you that I do nothing just to be polite.'

Sophie slipped her hand in his and he

pulled her to the centre of the garden, one strong arm around her. It was one thing to watch someone else dance, another to be standing there closer to any man she had been to before.

'It's rather simple really, we're making a square as we move. Just follow my feet backwards and they won't get stepped on. One . . . two. . . .'

Back, sideways, forward, sideways, each step she felt the soft caress of his breath on her ear. Sophie had never even seen her parents so intimate, only arguing, sniping, criticizing and here she was in the arms of little more than a stranger, one who had saved her life and knew of Jasper's shame, but a stranger nonetheless.

'What are the general objections, Miss Greenwood?' he asked, pulling her out of her concentration on not getting her feet stepped on.

'To what?'

'You said your mother called the waltz scandalous. I learned it in Vienna on a boyhood trip with my father, and it's been danced there for years. I'm wondering the reason for it being banned.'

She could certainly see the reason — any young man with a fancy to marry actually having the woman he admired in his arms.

No one to hear what he might say, or her for that matter? 'I believe the book Mama is always quoting states that the only people to dance it with propriety are husband and wife. She also read that it says there are very few women with whom men could bear to dance the waltz.'

'Everyone should marry someone with whom they couldn't bear to be alone then, is that what the book says?'

'I . . . uh. . . .' How could she say that it happened all the time, her parents were proof?

He started to smile at her reaction to such a question. 'Then, Miss Greenwood, if your partner has not stepped on your toes and knows what he's doing, he might just try to sweep you off your feet while you're too dizzy to know what's happening as he twirls you.'

'Well if you're going to be a proper instructor, you aren't going to neglect that part, are you?'

'Is that the dancing you mean, or the sweeping you off your feet?'

'Dancing, of course; if sweeping me off my feet is so *passé* that you warn me of it I shan't let you off easily in your instruction.'

A true smile took his mouth, none of the puzzling looks he once had. 'Decidedly well said.' His arm at her waist tightened slightly before he set them in a turn. Slowly they made their way around the garden, but after their first circuit and she caught the rhythm, he sped up with each revolution.

'Your mother's book was right: there are few women in the world with whom I could bear to dance the waltz. I'm not sure that makes it scandalous though.'

Maybe it was Lady Sandbourne's attempts but she couldn't imagine Mr Dyson not trying to matchmake as well. She wouldn't let him assuage his guilt by letting him repay her dowry, so was he trying to find her a husband? It wasn't so long ago that she had admitted she had hardly danced since she had been in London.

'Did Mr Dyson ask you to keep me from feeling sorry for myself?'

'He informed me who you were when I saw you with the Beresfords at the opera. I do like to know the names of the ladies I rescue from crazed men. I don't believe you came up in conversation otherwise.'

No mention of her not dancing. No mention of Mr Dyson's becoming sick just before the Easter visit. Perhaps Mr Dyson was doing it alone, perhaps it was just her imagination.

'Dear me, Sophie!' Mariah called from the

door. 'Aunt Sandbourne is coming this way. She says she's feeling faint from the heat inside.'

'I should be very vexed, Miss Greenwood, if you dance the waltz with anyone but me,' Mr Kittridge said quietly and, as if he had never been there, he vanished into the ballroom through the other door.

'I have never seen such a spectacle in all my days. Men and women in each other's arms. Every woman to whom the Almack's patronesses refused a voucher, was out there grabbing any man she could find. If anything so intimate as that . . . I mean, at least dance it with a peer . . . make the humiliation worth it,' Lady Sandbourne fumed, as her voice filled the garden. Sophie turned her back to hide the red in her cheeks at nearly being caught doing just that. 'Ah, Sophie, there you are, dear. You're a good girl for not falling into every fad that comes along, not that with your situation it would make things any worse.'

Sophie vanished back inside before she had to hear anymore.

Sophie could hardly keep her air of unconcern in check; she wasn't an unmannered girl and yet the longer she was in Lady Sandbourne's house the more she seemed

139

to want to defy her. Sophie wasn't ready to become a hoyden, but wanted to live life a little, to talk to people when she went out. She didn't want this snubbed half life, of digging the garden to avoid her mother. She had danced the waltz of all things, in defiance of Almack's earlier edicts.

But the freedom she felt fled when she walked into her room at the sound of Anjanette crying. She was holding a letter in her hand.

There was only one thing that came to mind that would bring Anjanette to tears: 'Jasper's dead?'

'No. I'm sorry, but I opened it when I saw who it was from. I couldn't help myself,' Anjanette managed before handing over the letter, the words making her crying worse.

Not dead. Then what?

Miss Greenwood
I still am not sure I can tell you truly what happened, why your brother was wounded after the battle was over. All we really know is that Private Halestrap went running at Jasper, bayonet aimed at his heart. Jasper fired in his own defence, but the gun exploded and shrapnel hit Halestrap in the leg. The bayonet hit but not as deadly as it could have done. Halestrap

was screaming about some man named Greyfriars as he attacked your brother. The rest of us rushed to Jasper's aid. We assumed Halestrap had been seriously injured, but by the time Jasper was seen to, Halestrap had vanished. We have caught Halestrap going through Jasper's pack several times since, but he runs off before we can get close enough. I hate to have to tell you this, but while the wound will heal, Jasper will probably be blind for the rest of his life. He's yet to wake, but with Halestrap still after him, we had to get him out of France. We were concerned Halestrap would go first to Rowengate. The fighting has unhinged his mind; he is quite mad now and we have no wish to unleash him on your family. Jasper's commission is sold as there is no hope of him continuing in his post. The money should be enough for some time. When the danger has passed you will find Jasper at the home of Private Croft in Polperro, Cornwall. Far from home, but in the circumstances we felt it was best for him. I am truly sorry I am the one to have to tell you of such news especially under such trying circumstances. If our fears come to pass, I would be very worried if Halestrap should come after you.

Yours Sincerely
Captain Andrew Willoughby

Sophie made a very quick decision. 'Anjanette, how can I get out of London without being followed? I can't very well go to Jasper if I lead the very man he is in danger of to him.'

'You would go now?'

'He's wounded, being cared for by strangers. How can I leave him there until some day when they might catch the fellow? The captain did a great deal to get him to safety, but I can't bear the thought of him just lying there, knowing his family haven't even come to his aid.'

'Have you funds enough to do such a thing?'

Sophie sat on the chaise chewing on her nail in thought. 'Hmm, Papa gave me some extra to spend here in London. I'll need a man's assistance though. That seems to be the only option. Could you imagine the fuss if it was found I had gone alone?'

'Mr Dyson?'

Sophie lifted her eyes hoping every thought in her head couldn't be seen. 'He's wealthy to be sure, but I think this needs a little more subterfuge. I think I should approach Mr Kittridge.'

Anjanette's eyebrow rose slowly. Before she said anything, though, she went to the window, hiding her face. 'Can I ask to come with you?'

Sophie stared at her back for a moment. 'Only if you aren't willing to come back. I was thinking of staying, but it would work much better if I was here to keep Halestrap distracted.'

Anjanette's smile grew slowly. 'You have no objections to me as sister?'

Sophie took a deep breath; she could hear her mother's objections already. 'He has asked you then?'

'I haven't hidden anything from you, Sophie. Jasper was intending to ask, but I do know, blind or not, I would still marry your brother tomorrow if he asked.'

Sophie nodded more to herself. 'I'll need to get a note to one of the men outside without being seen. He can pass it on to Mr Kittridge. Then we just have to concoct a reason to leave London that Lady Sandbourne will believe. If I'm thought to have run away, she could ruin this as much as Halestrap. The cry to find me wouldn't help keep Jasper hidden.'

Anjanette grinned. 'Perhaps Mrs Beresford is feeling unwell again?'

'Pure inspiration, Anjanette. Perfect.'

'There's a letter in the post for you, Sophie,' Mariah said, as she entered the drawing-room.

Sophie looked up quickly. Was it word that Jasper had died? 'From whom?'

'The return says Mrs Beresford.'

Sophie sighed with relief; it was Anjanette's letter written to give them a reason to leave. 'Thank you,' she replied, as Mariah handed it to her.

'You don't open it?' Lady Sandbourne asked.

'Oh, yes.' Sophie fumbled with the paper, worrying whether she could convince everyone she had no knowledge of the contents. 'Oh dear, Mrs Beresford is ill and asks that I come for a short stay.'

'Ill?' Lady Sandbourne questioned. 'She shouldn't call you to her side then and subject you to the same foul airs.'

'She's indisposed with a coming child. She's been quite ill to her stomach. That's why she didn't return to London.'

Lady Sandbourne wrinkled her nose. 'She could have planned things better. Not inconvenienced the *ton* at all if she was smart about it.'

'I may go to her then? A week wouldn't

ruin my season so much. It's not yet time for Ascot. I'll be back before that.'

Lady Sandbourne snorted impatiently. 'Not inconvenienced? Why, in the next week alone there are three balls, two routs, and I've not decided how many suppers we shall attend. There are invitations for some six. It is most inconvenient.'

Oh dear. Sophie silently implored Mariah for help. She hadn't expected there would be any opposition at all, but she was only Mariah's companion.

'This fellow who is following Sophie around though. If she was out of Town, it would be far safer for you to attend to your schedule as he would surely follow her,' Mariah said eventually.

Lady Sandbourne's eyes widened. 'Oh, of course, I hadn't thought of that, Mariah. This being followed about is most distressing. You should go, Sophie.'

'You aren't the one being followed,' Sophie muttered under her breath. It was time for them to dress for yet another visit though. Sophie quickly left the room before any other objections might arise. Before she could close her bedroom door behind her though, Mariah slipped in.

'Now what is that all about?'

'What do you mean?'

'Don't think you can pull the wool over my eyes like you have Aunt Sandbourne's. I know you, Sophie, far better than she. You've been jumping at everything since yesterday, even more than when that fellow half strangled you.'

Sophie took a deep breath. 'You can't tell your aunt. I have received a letter saying that Jasper has been injured. His men smuggled him aboard a ship to Cornwall to keep him safe from the very man who attacked me. I'm going to him. I can't just leave him there without his family around. Papa doesn't even know where he is. I had to make up this whole thing so that I could leave without this madman finding out I've gone to be with the man he already tried to kill.'

Mariah's hands flew to her mouth from the shock. For once her smiling eyes lost their sparkle. 'Should I come as well?'

Jasper was her cousin after all. 'No, I think if we all went away in the middle of the season, it would be too noticeable.'

'You'll take Anjanette and not me?'

'Unless you can tell me that you're all but engaged to my brother as well.'

Mariah looked back at the door and started to smile. 'It isn't surprising, I suppose.'

'I'll find a reason to leave Anjanette to care for Jasper so I can return and act once again as if I don't know where he is.'

'I'll send a letter to Phillippa asking her to put men at the gates again. You did say they did so when you were there? If he believes you are going there, it will keep up the fiction.'

'Thank you, Mariah.'

Sophie was drinking a cup of cinnamon spiced chocolate at breakfast with the others when Roberts announced Mr Kittridge. It had been days since Anjanette had managed to slip the note to his man on guard. Lady Sandbourne didn't care about Anjanette, who could come and go without being watched.

'I've told you not to admit him, Roberts. He's only trying to take advantage of Miss Greenwood's gratitude for his service to her,' Lady Sandbourne declared.

'What have you done?' Sophie demanded. 'Roberts, admit him immediately.'

'Sophie, there are far more deserving men of your affection.'

Sophie gritted her teeth at hearing he was being kept away. 'Roberts, now, please.' Lady Sandbourne said nothing as Sophie glared at her in the moment before Mr Kittridge entered.

'I hope I'm not interrupting,' he said, bowing his head. 'I've been trying to see you for several days, Miss Greenwood, but you haven't been at home.'

'And to what do we owe your presence today, Mr Kittridge?' Lady Sandbourne demanded. Albeit said pleasantly, it was a demand nonetheless.

'Miss Greenwood gave me permission to attend to a task for her. I came once more hoping I would find her at home.'

'You couldn't have sent word to give her some warning? A gentleman would have made the appointment at the lady's leisure,' Lady Sandbourne said, condescension in her voice.

That a marchioness was dressing him down did nothing to undermine Mr Kittridge's confidence; he even smiled faintly.

'Perhaps if she hadn't been kept so busy that she was seldom at home, it might have been done at her leisure.' Did he guess she had been there all along? That he had been stopped from seeing her?

Mariah gasped at his audacity. Surely, no one had ever spoken to Lady Sandbourne like that since she had married the marquess. 'Shall we go then, Mr Kittridge? I would hate Mrs Beresford to wait any longer,' Sophie announced, without care of offending.

'This would have been better done tomorrow though,' Lady Sandbourne said, half to herself. 'You don't have to be anywhere since Mariah attends Almack's tonight.'

Sophie could only stare as if her comments hadn't been said and she was leaving only at Lady Sandbourne's will. 'I believe I told you I must leave Town for a time. Mrs Beresford is feeling poorly and has asked that I come for a visit.' Sophie was almost to the stairs to get her trunk when Lady Sandbourne spoke again.

'Why doesn't Anjanette go with you? She'd only be bored here with you gone.'

Sophie smiled at a chaperon being forced on them just as they anticipated. If there was one thing that Sophie had learned of her hostess, it was that she would keep up conventions. Lady Sandbourne might as well have said she expected something to happen. She wondered, was it Sophie or Mr Kittridge that she didn't trust?

'Now what is this about?' Mr Kittridge asked, the moment they reached the carriage.

Sophie could only look out of the windows trying to spy Halestrap's unkempt blond hair. 'My brother, Mr Kittridge. We received word he's wounded by the same man who attacked me. We can't just leave him untended. Could you escort us to the coaching inn without my shadow finding out?'

Mr Kittridge glared at her for a moment. Would he refuse now that they had laid their plans so carefully? 'You can't tell me you're thinking of sneaking into France.'

'Heavens, no.' Sophie laughed, then dropped her voice to a mere whisper, even then not sure Halestrap might be lurking in the bushes waiting to hear. 'We received a letter from a captain that poor Jasper is blinded. He sold his commission and has sent him to Cornwall, to the house of a fellow soldier, to keep him safe while he heals. Only we have to leave Town without that dreadful man following us straight to my poor brother. Everyone thinks I'm off to visit the Beresfords again.'

Mr Kittridge rested his head back against the seat. 'Why not send him home?'

The pit of her stomach clenched with the thought. 'The letter said the captain didn't think it safe.'

'There's more than one of them,' he said quietly.

'What?' Anjanette shrieked.

'Have you been writing home to your family, Miss Greenwood?'

Sophie's hands went to her mouth. Indeed, how else would a man know she had been to Coverly Court? Following her would explain most but not all. The letters from Papa went to Lady Sandbourne's country house, not to the house in Mayfair. How would a man, wounded and stinking, learn anything from even the servants at Lady Sandbourne's or even Rowengate? The break-in would have given him the name Greyfriars. No, no, no Mr Kittridge was right. Jasper must have been observed writing the letter in France; Halestrap must know how to get to Rowengate in the first place.

'I haven't written of Jasper's wounds. It seemed something to do in person. Can you please take us to the coach?'

And then he smiled. With just that one bit of brightness, she might get through this horrid time. 'Well, since you said please.'

Sophie looked around when the carriage came to a stop. People were milling about everywhere. Once or twice she swore a shock of dirty blond hair peeked through the crowd. Would she never be free of him?

'This isn't the stop for the coach to Cornwall.'

'You said to help you get out of London without being followed. You're going to Mrs Beresford's, are you not? It's the coach to Coverly Court. Go inside the inn and empty your trunks. I need to speak to the driver.' Mr Kittridge climbed out of the carriage while the two of them still had no idea what was going to happen. Their brilliant plan was out of their hands. Still, there was a coach waiting, so their trunks were taken to the inn. They were shown to a side room and Anjanette rushed to pull the clothes from the trunks, handing them over for Sophie to put in little more than bags.

Only then did Mr Kittridge return to order them something to eat. The only protection they had was being surrounded by people. Still Sophie watched Anjanette constantly survey everyone. She worried about putting Jasper in danger even then. Mr Kittridge checked his pocket watch.

'The coach leaves in twenty minutes. The driver will wait in a position where you will able to get back inside here without being seen. Then go through the inn to my carriage; it will take you to Cornwall before the public coach leaves. I would suggest you keep your heads down until well away from here though.' That was all he said before he began to eat.

Perhaps if Anjanette hadn't been there, he might have filled the time with more than talk of the weather, this ball and that. All the while Sophie's stomach filled with dread that she might find her brother dead, or that she would lead Halestrap right to him and thus be the death of him. It would be bad enough if poor Jasper was gone; to add to her worry, Canmore Park would leave the family when Papa died and be settled on a cousin. All but Mama's £500 would be gone and without a house to live in and no food from the land. . . . Sophie forced the thought from her mind even if her stomach still churned. If they were alone, Mr Kittridge would have told some joke to take her mind off the inevitable, but Mr Kittridge had always been a gentleman. He would never say such things when another was there to hear how he flirted with a poor baron's daughter whom he called friend, flirted because she asked nothing of him.

The driver called from the door leaving Sophie and Anjanette to follow, several others stood in line behind them. No one said a word and her hands shook when they exited as soon as they were in, the whole commotion hiding the fact that more people than would fit had filed by. Before anyone could say a word, they were sitting in the same carriage in which they had arrived. Mr Kittridge did not go in though.

'You don't come with us?' Sophie asked, surprised.

'I've business I cannot avoid, I'm afraid. And yes, actual business, not just a falsehood to get out of something. Riordan will see you there.'

'Thank you, Mr Kittridge. You don't know what this means to me.' *Please let him live.*

'I've a brother too, Miss Greenwood. I imagine I do.' He motioned to the driver for them to leave. 'Stay down till you're out of sight.'

CHAPTER NINE

Cornwall was the furthest from home that Sophie had ever been. She had not been considered old enough before then, to make a trip further away from home than London. Coverly Court was in Essex, not much of a journey at all. It was no wonder she had worried of the expense of travel to visit Mariah: Scotland would far exceed anything she had contemplated until then. She hadn't seen the sea, the lakes, anything. She could speak Italian and French, but she hadn't set foot out of England, never sailed on a ship, never crossed the River Tamar into Cornwall. She hadn't crossed the desolate Bodmin Moor on the old route from Ireland to the Continent. All were places she had read about, nothing more. The fact that everyone she knew considered the Cornish people to be nothing more than taciturn smugglers. . . . Sophie started to laugh to herself. Miss Asquith was certainly taciturn, and although it was uncharitable to mention it, staring at her all night without a word qualified her as unsociable as well. *Please let him live.*

Anjanette shook Sophie's shoulder after days, it seemed, of sitting in the coach. 'Riordan says we're at Polperro.'

They swept round the curve of a hill, but when the hill faded away, a wide sheet of water stretched out before them. A cluster of cottages soon told of the start of the actual village. Scarlet rhododendron burst through the tree-covered hills while a breeze brought the unfamiliar smell of the sea.

Reaching the town centre, the driver slowed in front of an inn with the picturesque name of Nowhere Inn Particular. Someone had a sense of humour. Men stood about gossiping over their pipes, smoke curled from cottage chimneys all around.

'I'll go find out where your Private Croft's house is,' the driver announced, jumping down quickly. Riordan was a merry fellow who smiled with a particular sweetness, especially when it came to smiling at fair ladies. They'd seen it often in the last two days.

Sophie climbed out, unable to resist the

urge to look around. Ships were moored at the dock, nets spread out to dry on the cobbled streets after the fishermen's return. One lone fellow was still pulling crab pots from the sea. Much of the town was granite, quarried from the Cornish hills around them.

'No one will say a word, Miss Greenwood. I keep asking where to find Private Croft's house, but they just ignore me.' Riordan said in her ear, surprising Sophie from her reverie.

She was nineteen and could finally say she'd seen the sea. 'Then I shall go in and ask.'

Please let him live.

'Miss. . . .'

His words died away as Sophie entered the ancient stone building. Rustic and not a woman in sight, she could see the driver's reasons for trying to stop her. 'I'm looking for Private Croft's home? I imagine it is a simple enough question?'

No one said a word. One large man sat in the corner looking much different from the others who remained silent too; he stared at her in his refusal to help.

Why was she having images of Miss Asquith again? 'I'm here to find my brother. He's said to be staying at Private's Croft's home. Cannot one of you tell me where to find the house?'

No reply.

'Good day gentlemen. I just thought perhaps you might help me with a simple task, but if it troubles you so much. . . .' She turned to leave, tears threatening to fall. There was no doubt why Riordan hadn't tarried long.

'What's your name?' The gruff voice came from behind her just as her hand reached the knob.

'Miss Sophie Greenwood.'

'Last house on the lane, along the sea to the left.'

'Thank you, sir.'

Sophie felt like screaming as she walked out of the inn. Anjanette looked so hopeful though, Sophie just couldn't bring herself to upset her and so kept the scream bottled up. 'It is the last house on the lane, along the sea to the left.'

'Oh thank God,' Anjanette cried. Sophie climbed in the carriage once more and the driver hurried them along. A sea still as glass spread out beside them, but neither saw it on the fine bright day. Leaving the village proper, ferns covered the ground and bluebells were everywhere. Swallows darted about as their approach disturbed them.

Only Riordan's laughter broke the mood.

'What's the matter, Riordan?' Anjanette asked.

'Nothing, miss, I believe we've reached Croft's croft.'

The little joke helped remove the dread that was eating away at Sophie's stomach. There was no guarantee that Jasper still lived, only the news in an old letter written in France. The ivy-covered stone house was small, only five or six rooms. A slate roof and mullioned windows gave it a more prosperous look than many of the surrounding houses though, even if it still had a bare earth courtyard like all the rest. Lowing of cattle, rough voices, and the clanking of a pail told them that it was a farm despite being on the edge of the sea. A creaking iron gate was the only sound as they climbed down.

'Please let him live,' Sophie muttered to herself again, as she went to knock on the door. Despite the warmth of the day a shiver ran down her back.

'Go on in,' the same gruff voice called, before Sophie even had a chance to knock. Turning, they found themselves face to face with the large man from the inn. He grinned slightly at Sophie's astonishment. 'There's a shortcut from the pub if you're on foot.'

'Where's my brother? Where's Jasper?' Anjanette's hand squeezed hers tighter.

'Does he live?' Anjanette finally whispered.

'Alive, for now. He's only been awake a few times since he arrived. The wound needs help, more than my poor young sister can do. Mother was the healer. The letter telling my brother that Mother had died since he was here last could not have reached him.' He opened the door and led the way without another word. Upstairs, in a narrow bed, the room dark with drawn curtains, they found Jasper, pale, gaunt. He was half the man he had been the day he left for the army to help save their poor parents' money and to keep the rest of them fed.

Tears streamed down Anjanette's face as she rushed to Jasper's side. He groaned as she took hold of his hand. 'He's burning up.'

'Is there no surgeon to call?' Sophie demanded.

The man grunted. 'Aye, there is; never a bigger drunkard to be found in the whole county. I wouldn't risk making your brother worse calling him to his side. Ensign Greenwood's worse since he arrived. He was awake then. The army doctor had tended him well, but without that care since, he's

160

worsened.'

'Oh.' *Please let him live.*

'Is it true his sight is gone?' Anjanette asked, unable to look at them, her tears falling freely. Sophie doubted she would be able to see them even if she had looked.

'He could see some light when he was awake; I doubt he'll ever see properly though, miss,' Croft replied. Vincent Croft fed them supper; his sister showed them to a room, and through it all Anjanette cried. She had been awake for almost the entire trip. When presented with a bed and seeing that for the moment at least, Jasper still lived, Anjanette dozed. Sophie couldn't blame her, her eyes closed the moment she lay down as well.

Dawn woke Sophie early — the creaking gate, birds singing, the sound of the waves lapping on the cliffs only a dozen feet away. All, surely, sounds that didn't belong at Rowengate or Lady Sandbourne's house. Turning her head, the truth of where she lay came quickly. The realization that Anjanette was not in her bed came just as quickly. Sophie grabbed her wrapper and ran to Jasper's room. *Please let him live.* For a moment Jasper lay too pale, too still, before a deep breath eventually moved his chest. Anjanette wasn't there however. Vincent appeared at Sophie's side silently.

'He's well?' Vincent asked, his voice still tinged with sleep, her rush to Jasper's bed the only reason he had awakened.

'Anjanette isn't in our room. I thought she was here.'

'I've not heard anyone about.'

Anjanette had cried during the night before. As much as Sophie hated to think it, what came to mind was that Anjanette had returned home: Jasper wasn't the man she remembered.

'I'll go make some tea, miss.'

With the sun up high enough to truly see and awake enough to keep her eyes open, Sophie studied her brother. The wound was to his shoulder, no wonder he had groaned when Anjanette had taken his hand. His kind, pleasant face was tanned from the campaign on the Continent, and around the eyes especially his face was red from the gun that had exploded. It was the fact that he weighed so much less than he had that was the most noticeable change. Sophie and Jasper had the same colour eyes behind his closed lids. All the siblings did. They resembled each other only a little, but the eyes were the same.

As Vincent brought in the tea, Sophie realized how long she had been standing there. 'Did your brother know Jasper well then to send him to your home?'

The large man laughed faintly. 'We were well set up to receive him.'

'I don't understand.'

'I'll just say that you've probably heard what the Cornish coast is famous for. Lots of coves and bays for a man and ship to get lost in.'

Sophie still couldn't understand what on earth he meant. Her brow furrowed as she tried to puzzle it out. Cornwall was known for copper, granite, fishing and moors.

'Rum, miss, and lace, and a good many other things. Where do you think all things French come from with the war going on?'

For a moment she stared at him before it dawned on her — smuggling. She was staying in a smuggler's house. Lud, what a season she was having. Mama would have a fit.

'I have to be in town for the day; if you need anything my sister Margaret is about. In the barn, if you can't find her in the house,' Vincent said quietly.

'Thank you.' A week away wasn't going to be long enough. Jasper would not recover in that time.

■ ■ ■ ■

Mama had never taught Sophie anything that wasn't ladylike; even learning the healing properties of the plants in the garden would have been too much for her to know. She sat there, keeping a cool cloth to her brother's forehead unable to think of anything else. What should she do? She couldn't send Jasper home, couldn't move him, he was far too ill for that. Even moving his arm produced a groan of pain. Being rattled about in a carriage for hours might kill him. Could they put him back aboard a ship and sail him to the nearest large town where a proper surgeon could be found?

Please let him live.

With another fresh cool cloth in place, Sophie leaned back in her chair, exhausted. There by the bed was a bottle. It only contained water, but all Sophie could think of was that Vincent had talked about rum. Was Mr Kittridge involved in the dealings somehow? She had thought he seemed to have seen as much action as Jasper without having fought in a war. No, she couldn't start thinking such things. She'd be no better than Lady Sandbourne with her whispers of trade. Why should she care how he made his income? Pirated start or not, he was certainly steadfast when she was in need. Indeed, dare she use the word friend? As ill as everyone thought of her already, knowing a smuggler could not make things any worse.

The sun was setting, turning the sky a brilliant orange when Sophie heard the door opening downstairs.

'Vincent, could we get him aboard a ship to the nearest town of size that would have a surgeon?' Sophie called out.

'Sophie?'

The voice was quiet, but it was distinctly not Vincent or Margaret. Sophie turned to find Anjanette at the door. 'I thought you had left for good.'

'Fair weather or foul, Sophie.' Just the corner of her mouth curled up. 'I went to Plymouth to find a surgeon.'

Only then did Sophie catch the sound of wheezing following Anjanette up the creaking stairs. The surgeon was a portly fellow with a ring of white hair, but a pleasant smile at least.

'Now then, miss, how is the patient doing?'

Sophie felt tears coming to her eyes. She had assumed Anjanette had run off, but instead had gone for help. 'He's burning up and the wound is very ill indeed.'

'Well, perhaps you could find me something to eat. Miss Anjanette, here, dragged me off without my meal at noon and I will see what I can do for your brother.'

'Thank you.' It was dear Anjanette who helped Sophie make her way down the stairs.

Sophie rushed to Jasper's room when she woke hoping to find he still lived. All she could hear was the sound of her own blood pounding in her ears.

'You needn't have woken so early; he's sleeping soundly,' the doctor announced cheerfully.

'But has his condition improved at all?'

'He has not worsened, if that is your concern.'

Sophie took a deep breath. 'I have to return to London. The man who did that to him might get suspicious if I am gone any longer. Will he live?'

'It will be touch and go, miss, I will not lie to you.'

Sophie let out a sigh. 'Do what you can. That is all anyone can ask.' Walking back to her bed, Sophie slowly began to pack her things. She was returning to London but she didn't wish it. Not the way it was anyway. Whatever would she do? She couldn't keep Jasper hidden forever, if he lived that long.

Sophie watched in a daze as Vincent loaded the bags in the carriage.

'I'll take good care of him,' Anjanette said quietly.

Sophie couldn't find any words; she just hugged Anjanette, trying to keep the tears from falling. 'It's all I can ask,' she got out eventually.

'I'll send word if there's any change, one way or the other.'

'Sign it from Mother. She never writes, but no one else knows that.'

Anjanette smiled. 'I was talking to Vincent while you were sleeping, Sophie.' She pulled out a large package from behind her back, presenting it with a flourish.

'What's this?'

'French lace, some silk. Lady Sandbourne can't call your trip to see Phillippa a complete waste if you arrive with that.'

'I can't take this.'

Anjanette waved her hand as if it was nothing. 'It came out of the money from the sale of Jasper's commission. You know if he was awake, he would have done the same to see you married well. You know *I* would

167

do it to see him safe. No questions will be asked if you arrive bearing gifts.'

'You need to be going, miss.' Vincent interrupted.

CHAPTER TEN

Nothing had changed in London while she had been away. Lady Sandbourne would not have let it. Lud, a rake who had seduced more women than he could count would have more acceptance in society than Sophie did. A rake was smart enough not to try to push himself in aristocratic society, and yet that was just where Lady Sandbourne pushed Sophie every time she stepped out, the very society that would object the most. It was too bad Mr Dyson wasn't her sponsor for the season as she might actually have managed to dance. No one even noticed that she had left with a companion and had returned alone. No one seemed to notice either there were many new servants. There were no questions from Lady Sandbourne to indicate she even cared Sophie had been away, so there was no reason for Sophie to fawn all over a woman who cared nothing for her. So the gift of silk and lace she kept for herself. Inviolata raised an eyebrow, surely recognizing the French source of such fabrics, but said nothing as she listened to Sophie's request to create a gown for her and Mariah from it.

'Sophie, you're back!' Mariah cried, rushing in the room. 'Oh that is fine material, Sophie. Where did you find it?'

'There was a fellow in the village near Phillippa's house who said it was just off a smuggler's boat from France. Inviolata is to make a gown for both of us out of it.'

'Sophie, you're too kind.' Mariah gushed a bit and then turned to the dressmaker. 'Oh, could it be done before the Rivingtons' masked ball? What fun, we could dress alike. No one would know who was who.'

Inviolata smiled. 'I best get to work then. The colour would look delightful with a peacock's mask, don't you think?'

'Oh yes, of course, just the thing,' Mariah replied, clapping her hands in delight. With that, Inviolata withdrew and Mariah closed the door behind her. 'Don't leave me again, Sophie. I don't think I could bear it.'

'Whatever happened?'

'Wolfenway, of course; he's been here three times since you went away trying to hold my hand at every turn, and he perspires so. He even tried to peer down my dress.

How is Jasper?' Mariah asked quickly, turning the conversation away from the loathsome man.

'Very ill indeed. Anjanette found a surgeon to see him, but he's not certain he will recover. We can only pray.'

Mariah shook her head sadly. 'A leering wolf will keep you from worrying about him too much. He promised often to return when you came back.'

Sophie groaned at the thought.

'Mr Kittridge came to visit too. You can't imagine how badly Aunt Sandbourne treated him. She didn't even send word that she wasn't at home; she sent him away to his face before I could tell him you weren't returned yet.'

'Oh dear.' Who needed scandal when there were bad manners?

As Sophie rode in Hyde Park early the next morning, her horse shied but she wasn't so caught in thought this time. She easily took control of the animal before Halestrap suddenly sprang from the bushes.

'Tell me where Greyfriars —' he got out, but he had stepped too close by then and Sophie took her riding crop to him. The crop bit across his face so hard that he cried out, as she put her heel to the horse's flank.

She looked over her shoulder just long enough to see him slipping the grasp of the guard she had forgotten was following her every move.

When she caught sight of the man running after her, she slowed her horse allowing him to catch up once more.

'This way,' he murmured, taking the bridle of the horse. He swayed slightly as he walked, a sailor for certain still getting his land legs, but it was only as they left the main paths of the park that the fear returned.

'I don't even know you.'

'You going to take that crop to me, too? William'd have my hide if anything happened to you.'

'Would he now? He might as well be taking me to an inn and having his way with me if talk like that got abroad. I'm thought a fortune hunter; I don't need London thinking I'm a Cyprian too.'

The man smiled up at her. 'If you was, miss, I'd be a certain customer and Lady Sandbourne's is straight up the street here. I'll make sure you're not followed.' He slapped the horse's flank and she trotted off, hardly aware of the fact that no man had ever spoken to her with such impertinence. No, what was she saying? Offers of *carte blanche* were much worse and those who made them were serious in such things. This man was no more than jesting with a woman he found attractive.

As Sophie dressed for dinner, the maid brought in a note for her. Another girl she had not seen before.

'Lady Sandbourne isn't very happy about you receiving notes from men. She wants to know if there is an engagement she should know about,' the maid announced. Sophie took the paper without a word though. Short and to the point, Mr Dyson was inviting her to dinner and the opera with him and his wife Wednesday next. A night free from sitting at home while Almack's was barred to her.

'Mr Dyson and his wife invite me for dinner. Make sure my silver gown is ready for Wednesday evening.' She wasn't in the mood to be polite to the servants just then. The implication that she would run off with a man, couldn't be trusted in a carriage alone, and made engagements to who knew what rake Lady Sandbourne imagined, did not make her feel a welcome guest. She was an entertainment nothing more, as she had always known.

The next day Sophie entered the drawing-room to find Mr Beresford there taking tea. An MP was obviously worthy of being admitted and seated in the best room. She couldn't imagine how Mr Kittridge could see her as a friend any longer after such horrid treatment from Lady Sandbourne.

The first thought that came to her mind when they announced him, was, 'Is Phillippa unwell?'

At that he smiled. 'Oh, of course she is well. A friend of mine was held up and asked if I would take you to an appointment you just cannot miss.'

What was he talking about? She had no engagements that she recalled. 'What engagement is that?'

'I was told you desired to find out about your brother. The man to ask has been tracked down at last.'

Narrowing her eyes, Sophie tried to discern what he meant and the only answer that came to mind was Mr Kittridge. He had mentioned once about finding out information about her brother, but that was before she had seen Jasper in person. She had assumed he would put the offer aside.

'Where are we going?'

'I was told to deliver you to Horse Guards in Whitehall.'

'And Lady Sandbourne agrees?'

Everard smiled devilishly. 'The marchioness is out visiting with your cousin, so I was told.'

Yes, of course, to the women who wanted Lady Sandbourne to visit, but not her. There had been mention of an errand, but not that she was being excluded from actual visits.

'I'll get my hat.'

Sophie's stomach boiled with dread as the carriage made its way through the city. She didn't need to have proof her brother was invalid and a thief, but that she hadn't heard from Anjanette worried her more, even if it had only been a few days; no letters was not good.

'Seventy-seventh Regiment of Foot, you said?' Mr Kittridge asked through the window and she jumped.

Sophie hadn't even noticed they'd stopped. 'Yes.' It came out little more than a whisper. She alighted from the carriage and Everard sent the driver on, leaving them there on the pavement. Her eyes roamed looking for the dirty blond-haired Halestrap to attack again. Then the reality that she was truly alone with a man without a chaperon in the middle of London hit her. Staying with Vincent Croft, she'd felt no such feeling, Jasper was there, even if not awake to say anything: his presence was felt.

'How is your brother? I've been unable to visit and find out how your adventure fared,' he asked quietly.

Could he read her mind like a gypsy? 'Alive the last I saw him, but barely. Anjanette stayed to see to his care; she'll send word if there's any change.'

He raised an eyebrow. 'You'd leave his care to another?'

Sophie tried to think of how vague her answer could be. She wasn't one to ruin a woman's reputation, especially when it concerned her own brother.

'Like that, is it?'

Sophie looked up; her silence was answer enough. 'It seems there was an attachment before he left for the army. No promises were made, but her feelings have not changed for him, even though he is wounded.'

'Take a deep breath, it will all work out well.' Mr Kittridge added.

'And if he is thief? He is my only brother. My father is elderly, and two sisters are not even fourteen. I hate to say how much we live on as it is. With no house or estate, it will have to pay for far more. There will be scandal if he lives — even worse, poverty if he dies.'

'Why don't you restrain your gloomy thoughts until you know for certain? In an hour you might laugh at all this worry, so save yourself the exertion of it now.'

'I've been so worried imagining the worst, even more so since that fellow came at me in the park. To think I might not have been able to find out even this if Lady Sandbourne had kept up her campaign. I don't need to guess why you sent Mr Beresford to collect me.'

Standing at a door as a man opened it for them, Sophie looked at Mr Kittridge, who seemed unfazed at the thought. 'You don't mind that she holds such prejudice against you?'

She received a smile at that. 'No, the fantasies of a bored marchioness don't concern me at all. But you do, which is why Mr Beresford did me a favour and kidnapped you from the house.'

A soldier led them in to where a man stood quickly, brilliant in his scarlet uniform faced with yellow. He was older but still surely tanned from being on campaign.

'This is the young lady looking after her brother then, Mr Kittridge?'

'Miss Greenwood, may I introduce Captain Andrew Willoughby, Captain in the Seventy-seventh.'

'Then you know my brother?' Sophie asked abruptly. She'd not expected to be led to someone so close to Jasper. Perhaps some clerk in the bowels of the building who kept the records and would have a list, not a man who had actually served with him.

'Quite well, Miss Greenwood. He's a good man, lacking in reason now and then, but not lacking in courage. Always in the thick of battle. He was commended several times before he was wounded this last time and sold out. Do be seated. What is it you wish to know? I assume the letter about his wounds reached you.'

'You sent the letter? You helped get him out of France then?'

Captain Willoughby smiled at her like a father with his child. How many letters like that had he written? Finally, she would get answers.

'Have you any clue as to what is going on? This Halestrap attacked me even before I received your letter.' Mr Kittridge only nodded in agreement leaving it all to her. Had she ever been allowed to lead a conversation when there was a man in the room?

'Goodness. We sent the letter to you thinking you would not be affected. It was your home we thought would be watched.'

'I'm guessing, but I think there is another involved keeping watch on the house. There was a burglary and Miss Greenwood seems to be in danger no matter where she goes,' Mr Kittridge added.

The Captain grew angrier. 'What a mess. Yes, our Private Thomas Halestrap was starting to show signs of instability after Vitoria, we assume brought on by the fighting. Before it became noteworthy though, he vanished, we believed with pilfered spoils from Vitoria, never to be heard from again, until that day he attacked Jasper. Is there any word on his condition?'

Sophie shook her head. 'The last I saw him he was very ill. I chose to come back to keep Halestrap's attention on me and not elsewhere.'

'I've seen the man myself. He seems to be following Miss Greenwood. She was half strangled earlier in the season and he's popped up several more times, but he hasn't been able to cause as much damage since,.' Mr Kittridge added.

Captain Willoughby's grey eyes widened.

'I'll put out word that he's around. He is a deserter after all. I'll see if we can't spare some men to stand guard duty at your lodgings, Miss Greenwood.'

'His leg is putrid, if that helps to identify him. Jasper is so ill from his wound, I can't see how Halestrap can bear his. I might not recognize his face if he shaved, but his smell is very distinct.'

'I'll ensure a report is filed immediately.'

Sophie had to know how much trouble Jasper had brought on their heads, but how? 'Captain Willoughby, would this Private Halestrap be in trouble for taking spoils from the French wagons? Is he a thief, or just a deserter? How desperate a creature am I dealing with?'

The captain laughed heartily. 'Spoils of war, Miss Greenwood, nothing more. Most of the men sold what they took to the local Spanish for ready coin, which disappeared readily enough on drink and gambling. It's his lunacy I'd worry about.'

A knock on the door brought a man asking for Captain Willoughby's presence.

Sophie knew all she needed to know. 'I won't take up any more of your time. I'm grateful beyond belief to learn what you've told me,' she announced, as she readied to leave. 'Thank you, Captain, thank you.'

Sophie rose as the man waited by the door. Mr Kittridge was already halfway out when Sophie turned on a whim at a thought entering her head. 'Captain Willoughby, there isn't anyone in your offices here or in the regiment named Greyfriars is there?'

'I'd remember that name, but haven't come across it before.'

The moment the door closed behind them, Sophie threw her arms around Mr Kittridge's neck. No more scandal would tarnish their name. At the sound of a cough, though, she realized what she had done. Letting go quickly, she saw an old veteran at a desk.

'My brother is alive,' she lied to him. The fellow smiled and went back to his work.

'See, you worried for nothing,' Mr Kittridge murmured, as they made their way back out.

Sophie felt a blush cover her face. 'Do forgive my display.'

He grinned widely and a most ungentlemanly wink followed. She'd thought once Mr Kittridge was no love-struck boy, but he sometimes watched her as if trying to fathom something he saw in her. 'I rather enjoyed it, to tell the truth.'

'You found him just so that I could discern if Jasper was a thief.'

'That is what friends do. I rather suspected he wasn't, but I didn't think you would believe me if I just said so.'

Finally, Sophie got up the courage. 'Why do you stare so, Mr Kittridge? Do I offend?' She asked, as he helped her into his carriage. She took the hand he offered to help her, and he didn't let go after she was seated.

'Offend? Heaven forbid. I've been trying to decide how you've caught the colour of the seas of Jamaica in your eyes. I thought I should miss the sight until I returned home, only to find it looking at me with far more life than I ever saw in the ocean.'

Sophie felt her heart stop. That certainly didn't sound like uninterested flattery to her jaded ears. Was Phillippa right? Did he flirt for more than just to pass the time of day? No, it was impossible even to think about.

'Mr Kittridge, with compliments like that, it's no wonder Lady Sandbourne makes up excuses to keep you away. You must worry her you'll run away with me.'

'Why should I do that? If I made you an offer, I'd fully respect you enough to have your hundred pounds settled on you. I might come from a pirate background, but a gentleman could never live down being thought after a woman's money.'

After the relief of hearing Jasper was not a thief, there was nothing to weigh down her laughter.

Sophie sank into Mr Dyson's carriage when it arrived. Escape! Even if only for an evening. Lady Sandbourne had been quite overbearing since her return. She'd thought that before — escape — hadn't she? And she'd only been in London a few days this time.

'Sophie, I'm not sure you remember my wife. She was in the country when you came for dinner last.' Mrs Dyson was a spry-looking woman. Despite her age, her hair was still jet black and deep-green eyes sparkled with a smile that filled her whole face.

'Not really. I don't think I've seen you since I was twelve. I don't remember Mrs Dyson coming with you often.'

'No; I visited your family with John often until the boys were born, five in as many years takes up much of a woman's time. We didn't have the funds to hire a governess as we would now either,' she chirped brightly. 'Call me Anne.'

'Five boys? You aren't in the marriage market are you Mrs Dyson?'

'Heavens, no,' Anne exclaimed. 'The oldest is but sixteen.'

'Good, I was looking forward to a night away from such matters.'

Anne's chuckle filled the carriage. 'Well then, my child, what else is left to speak of?'

'No one's paid you any particular attention?' Mr Dyson asked. 'You've always been a famous local beauty.'

Was that the task of all long married couples? To find entertainment in the unmarrieds lack of the same? 'I've hardly danced with three men the whole time I've been in Town, and one is only doing so to hide that he's pursuing my cousin.'

Anne clapped her hands prettily. 'Oh, we shall have to rectify that immediately, Husband.'

Sophie gave Mr Dyson a pleading look. 'Dancing isn't the issue,' she murmured quietly, as if reminding herself of the reason she hardly danced.

'No, Mrs Dyson, we've plans for dinner and the opera. I believe Miss Greenwood has been without such simple entertainment since her friend went back to the country. Balls the like of which she is taken to every evening, I would certainly find tedious.'

'Do you speak Italian then?' Anne asked, changing the subject.

'Yes, I had a tutor for some years.'

'Delightful; then you can tell me what we hear. I've never had an ear for languages.'

At that Sophie had to laugh. 'I've not practised in several years. If I falter, please don't reprimand me.'

'My dear, how shall I know?'

Sophie laughed, until she caught sight of Halestrap, but the carriage pulled away before he could get close enough to reach her. Still, the last image she had of him was his lunging at the carriage trying to grab hold. He ran off as she saw one of Mr Kittridge's men closing in on him. Would it never end? Would she not even be free of him when she returned home to Rowengate? Her walks to escape her mother's tongue would come to an end. He already knew a way in; he had ransacked the house even. Father had spoken of it in his letter. Because her brother could be thought a thief, there could be no hue and cry to catch the man who followed Sophie relentlessly.

Anne's warm hand clasped hers. 'Are you ill, Miss Greenwood? I swear all colour just left your countenance.'

The shops were filled with people bustling everywhere. Lady Sandbourne and Mariah had dropped Sophie off before going for lunch with some titled man who was interested in Mariah, it seemed. Mariah would pretend interest in anyone as long as it wasn't Wolfenway and it saved an altercation with her aunt.

Looking at some unusual sheer fabric, Sophie would have sworn she felt someone watching her. There wasn't a man in sight though, Halestrap especially. A man, she assumed was one of Mr Kittridge's guards, could be seen loitering outside the window. Moving on, she found a beautiful silk that would set off her colouring exquisitely. She asked the attendant to cut her the amount for a dress. There was only so much she could endure of knowing she was wearing the hand-me-downs of a woman who cared so little about her. Just as she went to pay, someone bumped her arm.

'Excuse me.'

Sophie spun, her heart in her throat that somehow it was Halestrap. No man trying to kill her stood there though. It took a moment to recognize the woman, she was one of Lady Sandbourne's maids. *What was her name again?*

'Tilly, does the marchioness need me? I thought they were to lunch with the duke.'

'She let me go, Miss Greenwood.'

Only then did Sophie notice her arms

were full of bolts of fabric. 'What? Why?'

'I don't rightly know. I wasn't even paid before she threw me out, without a recommendation to find another position as maid. I've taken a place here, but the wage is a quarter of what it was with her. I don't know how I'll manage.'

It was impossible not to see the tear running down the woman's cheek. It was even harder not to see the connection to the new maid who had brought her the note. Tilly had been one of the most conscientious servants Sophie had come across in the house. There was no reason for her to be dismissed.

'Could I have some of that beige you're carrying?' It would work well as a coat, with a matching hat perhaps. It would give her a reason to talk to Tilly apart from the others.

'Of course,' she said slowly. With a sigh she carried it over to an empty counter.

Sophie looked around carefully. She didn't know why, but she believed a girl she had hardly said a word to more than she would a marchioness. 'I know it won't make up for what happened, but I can at least give you the wages you were denied.'

'No, miss, I'm not looking for charity.'

'You earned it, so it's not charity. You were serving me, it's for the help you gave me.'

Sophie knew how it felt to be given charity, she had had two years of it. Her season in London was charity. A maid's wages weren't much, she knew, but everything helped when you had nothing.

'Thank you, miss,' Tilly whispered quietly, as she cut the fabric.

Taking it, Sophie slipped the money to Tilly so no one could see.

'Shall I send a bill?'

'No, I'll pay now. I'm here until I'm collected and who knows when that will be. They are lunching with a duke.' That was one thing her father was adamant about. They might not have any money, but they weren't in debt. He considered that a far greater scandal than poverty.

'The one she owes money to?' Tilly asked.

'I wouldn't know.'

'He was calling almost daily for close to a month before I left; he's not very happy with her. He covered some gambling debts of hers and she's yet to pay him back.'

Now that was interesting. 'Really?'

Tilly stiffened. 'There's some bolts in the back that were damaged a little, more than anyone paying full price would like to see, but you mentioned you had younger sisters not out yet. They could cover the flaws nicely with their embroidery.'

Sophie looked over her shoulder and saw the manager, or someone of importance, standing near. 'Of course, what an excellent idea. You're quite right, my sisters would love something new. Can I see what you have?'

Tilly led the way to the back, where there were five bolts of fabric, all as expensive as any in the shop.

'Even half of that, I can't afford.'

'I can't be seen talking to the customers, I'll get in trouble.'

'Do you have damaged fabric though?'

'Oh yes. I can get it if you really want to look.'

Sophie grinned. 'Then you can talk and not get into trouble.' And that was how Sophie learned that Mariah had been sneaking out to meet Mr Fraser in the street. His aunt lived just a few doors down, and they would meet each other while saying they needed some fresh air. She also discovered Inviolata used to be the mistress of some French aristocrat, but had to flee when the Revolution started. Her lover was one of the first killed. She'd been the man's wife's seamstress. It was also how she managed to buy five bolts of fabric for ten shillings apiece, enough to make her sisters an entire new wardrobe.

Sophie inspected the material spread out on her bed. The damage wasn't too serious. Tilly was correct, though, no one would want to pay full price from such an exclusive warehouse. For the first time in two years, her sisters could have something that wasn't the cheapest to be found in the village. After wrapping up the marerial, she wrote a letter, neglecting the news of Jasper, in case the watcher at home got hold of it. Turning back to the bundle on her bed, Sophie grinned as she stared at the nondescript package. A bundle sent home would cause much curiosity. There were those looking for treasure, she would give them some. Only one detail remained: how to set her plan to motion. She had to approach one of Mr Kittridge's men without Halestrap becoming suspicious.

The odious Viscount Wolfenway of Wolfenhame End came to visit four times in as many days. That meant four times Sophie and Mariah were just on their way out to go shopping even if they weren't planning to until he arrived. While there were hats, gloves, shoes, fans, parasols and such, to be found ready made, the rest required them to go back for final fittings. There were excuses enough to keep from sitting down with the man for an entire month if need be. But when Lady Sandbourne led them into a room with the very man in the midst of a group of people, it wasn't so easy to avoid the situation.

'Ah, Miss Greenwood, Miss Randolph, let me escort you into dinner,' Viscount Wolfenway called brightly, as soon as dinner was announced. Sophie felt the goose bumps down her arms or was that chills from the look he gave them? It was impossible not to notice Mariah pulling her fichu closer at the neck to deflect his leering glances at her bosom. It was one thing to be in Town for the marriage market; it was another to be on display like a side of beef hanging in the butcher's.

Sophie stared instead down at the table. There was oyster sauce, fish, spinach, fowls, soup, bacon, two kinds of vegetables and roasted beef for the first course. It kept her tongue from telling the man to unhand her that minute. Fortunately, he wasn't seated near either of them. Mariah was nearer the foot of the table flanked by Sir Ashley Halls and a Mr Linden. Sophie was opposite, with Lord Worthington on one side but the other seat was vacant. Constantia wine was being poured as everyone found their seats. It was a small dinner party, no more than twenty.

Lady Sandbourne was at the foot of the table and their host, Lord Woodruffe, at the head.

'Do forgive me, I'm late it seems. Business I just couldn't avoid.'

Sophie closed her eyes when she heard Mr Kittridge's voice break the murmurs. The chills the viscount's manner caused seemed to vanish. A friend at last.

'Ah, business means a woman, I take it?' Lord Woodruffe laughed.

'Actually there was a problem with a shipment; I had to rush to the docks to attend to it.' Mr Kittridge answered, as he took his seat next to Sophie. Had she noticed she would have seen his name was on the card, but with the viscount staring her senseless, she had been far too preoccupied. Lady Sandbourne mouthed the word trade to her nearest dinner companion.

'We seem to keep running into each other, Mr Kittridge,' Sophie said, hiding her mouth in her glass; she didn't like Lady Sandbourne watching every conversation she had.

'I've yet to hear you complain I'm in trade, so I haven't taken to avoiding you yet.'

So he had seen the same exchange she had. Other than the fact that he was free to do as he wished, Sophie wasn't quite sure why the quote came to her. He was no prisoner. ' "O'er the glad waters of the dark blue sea, Our thoughts as boundless, and our souls are free".'

'I'm surprised your mother allows Byron in the house.' For a moment, he looked at her. 'Then again, a man is the head of his house, is he not?'

Sophie couldn't help but smile. 'He's one of Father's favourites.'

'Mr Kittridge, will you be attending the Rivingtons' masked ball next week?' Lady Sandbourne asked loudly.

'No. I'm to be away for a sennight on business.' He took his glass of wine and turned away from Lady Sandbourne's gaze. Mr Kittridge looked to be pondering for a moment. His next words came as a whisper for only Sophie. 'George is the man in charge of those keeping watch. If you have need of anything, just shout for him and they will be there. It isn't so obvious as their following you, but it's time Halestrap's actually caught instead of just being run off. They are the crew from my ship. No better men in the Atlantic in a fight, and they are just sitting idle until we fill the hold again. They have only to get their hands on him.'

'Thank you, Mr Kittridge.'

Lady Sandbourne hardly let him get a word in after that though. All through the first and second courses, she kept asking him questions the moment it seemed he might try to say anything to Sophie. Lord Worthington ignored her though, if that was the purpose of not letting Mr Kittridge take up her time.

'You seem to have an admirer,' Mr Kittridge said quietly, as Lady Sandbourne was caught in an argument with her neighbour over who had the best iced cakes.

Her eyes immediately turned to where Viscount Wolfenway was sitting near to Lady Sandbourne. How had she ever thought the staring made him feel like meat in a butcher's shop? As Mariah said, he was a wolf, like his name suggested, and she was a sheep. 'Unwanted admiration, I assure you. I don't imagine he would be so easily scared off by threatening him with your men like Halestrap. The real issue is if I deter him, there is Mariah for him to latch on to. We aren't really certain for whom he is meant.'

Mr Kittridge looked over at the man. Viscount Wolfenway still stared as if no one cared he wasn't being correct in his manners. 'I think I see why you are rather bitter about having people thrown at you.'

'Mr Kittridge!' Lady Sandbourne called, now that her iced cake debate was resolved and she noticed their conversation.

'Lady Sandbourne?'

'What sort of trade is it that you engage in again?'

Sophie tried not to groan at such a blatant attempt to make him seem inferior to everyone there. He was the only one who did not bring up Sophie's situation, so she was willing to defend him endlessly. That his flirting was all the levity she had had since coming to London, she felt she might very well give Lady Sandbourne a set-down. Mr Kittridge though, only smiled as if nothing mattered, as if Lady Sandbourne was the one beneath them all for bringing up the subject.

'Rum and sugar, late of Jamaica. We've a plantation there called Aintree.'

'Now you sell yourself —' Lord Woodruffe muttered.

Mr Kittridge called over the butler, stopping Lord Woodruffe mid sentence. 'I forgot that I had brought a case of my finest stock for Lord Woodruffe. Could you send someone to my carriage? The driver knows where it is.'

'Of course.'

'Good man, Kittridge. Have several bottles

made into rum punch, Farley, and we'll have it as an end to our meal,' Lord Woodruffe called, as the butler left.

'I have just been told you have written a rather odd will; what was it again?' Lady Sandbourne asked, getting back into the conversation.

'It stipulates that in order for any descendant of mine to inherit, they must serve aboard one of our ships and for a period of not less then five years. Only then would they inherit.'

Several of the women gasped. 'You mean no higher education? How barbaric!'

'And what does that create? A boy who, having been given it without restriction, never learns the value of a pound. The gaming hells are filled with such boys who never work a day in their lives. You make laws to forbid them from ever selling their estates, forcing them to marry for the sake of money to prop up the family name until the next one marries more money.'

Lady Sandbourne sniffed in disdain. 'I suppose you've not set foot in a gaming hell then, or a university?'

'I don't claim to be a saint, or uneducated, only that I had to learn the value of what I was given, and those after me will as well. If I lose my shirt gambling, it's not at the cost of those coming after me.'

'You've children then?' another asked.

'None.'

The arrival of the rum punch stalled Lady Sandbourne for a little while as everyone was served.

Taking a healthy drink after she received her glass, Lady Sandbourne settled her gaze not on Mr Kittridge but on Sophie. 'You make it sound as if you would even marry my house guest here. She's destitute — you can't imagine the scandal her mother caused — wearing my cast-off clothes just so she doesn't appear in rags. Is Sophie the type you will look for in order to have children who will work to inherit what little you've scraped together?'

'Aunt!' Mariah cried. Her face was as red as possible, the laughter in her eyes vanished.

The other guests at the table, regardless of whether they knew the truth or not, had the decency to look horrified at such words. Lady Sandbourne just sat there grinning at the entertainment.

Mr Kittridge drank his entire glass in one gulp before standing. 'If finding someone poor, and yet born to a titled name like Miss Greenwood, would produce children with correct manners, I'd certainly pass by a child from someone who had only married into a title yet had money. The difference in upbringing certainly tells. Ladies, if you would care to retire, the gentlemen and I can enjoy our brandy. I found a box of cigars when I was inspecting the ship, gentlemen. Some of the finest in the West Indies, if anyone would care for one.' He looked only briefly at Sophie before the ladies rose and left the room. His mouth was in a grim line, but she swore he gave her an ungentlemanly wink as she went.

Lord Worthington was hooting loudly. 'Well said, Kittridge, manners certainly don't come cheap.'

After several cups of rum punch watered down for the ladies, Sophie began to feel the effects. Just enough so that things were a little hazy around the edges. Sophie had avoided Lady Sandbourne's gaze, and she had grown tired of waiting for the next cut and retire to the balcony which overlooked a wonderful garden illuminated by a full moon. It must be the rum affecting her, but Sophie briefly imagined herself as the hostess of the dinner that night even as the tears fell down her cheeks. It was something she knew would not happen. Her mother would preside over her for years to come. A house of her own, like Phillippa's, would not be hers. She would live in her parents' home, and then Jasper's if he lived. The stigma might be forgotten by the time her sisters were old enough to marry, but when that day came, Sophie would be an old maid, or someone's companion. She could only hope those in the future would treat her with more respect than using her troubles for the sake of entertainment.

'Ah, here you are.' The voice was fuzzy, like her vision. Arms folded around her and hot breath grazed her ear. 'You're a fine-looking woman, you know that. One who could certainly make a man's evenings more enjoyable.' Lady Sandbourne's shrill laugh filtered through from the drawing-room. Sophie wasn't the only one feeling the rum punch.

Another voice filled the balcony. 'I believe the last man to make such an offer was beaten by those protecting her.'

Ah, that was Mr Kittridge's voice, so who had his arms around her? Sophie watched as the arms vanished. She turned just in time to see Viscount Wolfenway disappearing inside. Her skin crawled at the thought.

'Are you all right, Miss Greenwood?'

His jaw was covered in stubble again, his piercing blue eyes stood out more than she could remember anyone else's ever had. Somehow, she couldn't pull her eyes away from them. 'You sound positively unaffected by all the liquor we've been plied with,' she said stupidly, but it was the only thing that came in her head at the moment. Mr Kittridge's laugh washed over her and the chill of Wolfenway's touch left quickly. He still smiled as he reached to wipe away the tears from her cheeks. Her breathing almost stopped.

'That punch isn't strong enough to get my ten-year-old cousin in her cups and I'm no child. I'll send a case over for you to get used to it. We can't have you taking up any offers a man makes you when you aren't able to think straight after a single glass with dinner.'

Sophie wasn't sure why her heart wouldn't calm down. All she knew was just then she wanted to be kissed. Her first and last kiss had been when she was fifteen. A neighbour, now dead in the war with France, had asked it of her before he left to enlist, before her father thought her old enough to be in danger of men after her dowry. Before she was considered a woman. Four years now she had been so well guarded that she had not met anyone alone and then . . . and then . . . no one cared to know her.

'I'm surprised Lady Sandbourne even let Mariah and I drink any. She dictates everything else in our lives.'

Mr Kittridge stood so close to her as she looked out over the garden that she could feel the heat of his arm through her clothes. 'But a drunken chaperon isn't much of a chaperon at all. I could run away with you and she'd never even know.'

Sophie couldn't help but look up, grinning at the man who had saved her life. 'Are you planning such a thing? I know, you've heard Lady Sandbourne gave me a thousand pounds and you want to get your hands on it. I'll have to see my solicitor post haste and make sure my fortune is secure.'

The jest left his face. 'Why would she do that?'

'In case she can't find me a husband, I'll have some funds of my own to be able to visit friends and family without asking for charity. I was worried when Mariah started to show interest in a man with an estate in Scotland, that I should never see her again. The longer I'm in Town the more I think the keeping of it has a higher price that its value on paper. After tonight I think she's certainly making me pay.

'Then why not return it?'

'I spoke of it as mine and yet I've never

seen it, nor what bank it is in. Once she offered to put it in the bank that was the last
time she mentioned it. Perhaps it is just
another of her jokes in regard to my feelings. The fact that I have no dowry seems
to entertain her greatly.'

For a moment, Mr Kittridge stared as if
unable to comprehend such a statement. 'Is
no one truly rich enough to be able to take
you without a dowry?'

Sophie snapped, a little annoyed he still
didn't seem to fully grasp her situation, 'If
they have enough that it doesn't matter,
they think me a fortune hunter, remember?
And when I am with Lady Sandbourne, she
turns away anyone who doesn't meet her
standards. That leaves only men who . . .
how exactly am I supposed to believe anything other than I shall be a spinster for the
rest of my days? I would rather that than
forego all my own beliefs and take up with
some man offering nothing more than —'

There, in the middle of her speech, she
was being kissed, nothing like the boyish attempts of the neighbour when she was
fifteen. Sophie was never going to smell bay
rum again without such thoughts entering
her head. Not with memories of his hands
caressing her shoulders, the whole of him
strong against her, his stubbled face rasping

against her cheeks — the sound of the door opening. Slowly Sophie opened her eyes as Mr Kittridge took a deep breath.

His smile grew quickly. 'And now you can say you've been kissed just to shut you up,' he murmured, before stepping away from her. 'Not quite spinster then perhaps.'

'Ah, here you are, William,' Lord Woodruffe called loudly. There was no doubt he had far more of the punch than anyone. 'You have to come tell us more tales of the West Indies. The ladies are leaving, but the gentlemen are loath to go.'

'Good evening, Miss Greenwood, sleep well,' Mr Kittridge said with a twinkle in his eyes before Lord Woodruffe grabbed his arm and pulled him along.

'What was that tale you mentioned from the year eight . . . ? Pirate smugglers.'

It was all Sophie heard before Lady Sandbourne came and whisked her away. At two in the morning the marchioness finally remembered her place as chaperon, horrid though she was at it. Two in the morning and Sophie could only think that her first real kiss might be her last. She'd rather dwell on that than meet Lady Sandbourne's eye on the ride back.

At last, a maid delivered a letter from the

post. It was from her mother who had yet to send word to her at all. For a woman who was determined Sophie should get a husband, she showed a marked lack of curiosity. Or did she believe, like all of London, that there was no chance? Sophie ripped open the seal to find Anjanette's careful penmanship.

Dear Sophie

I know you would have wished news sooner, but I wanted to make sure that the danger had passed. The surgeon finally smiled. Jasper lives without a fever. He has not woken yet, and is still very weak, but I am told he will make a full recovery. Even if he may never regain his sight, he will be able to speak to us soon and clear up this confounded situation once and for all. I won't write much; I know Lady Sandbourne will have you running all about London, but you can know your brother is well on his way to recovery.

Mother

It took two more days before the opportunity arose and she could talk to one of Mr Kittridge's men. The fact that she could have told Mr Kittridge himself when they were at dinner had vanished from her mind altogether. The whole evening had been too distressing to think about it.

She had tried catching sight of one of the men, but they weren't being as obvious as before. It took Halestrap's attempt to attack her once more as she walked down the street with Mariah.

'Someone, help!' Mariah screamed, as Halestrap knocked her to the ground.

Sophie hadn't even seen him before he was right there. He was certainly getting more daring. Mr Kittridge was right, he needed to be caught quickly, but without having ten men following her making it obvious to a blind man that they were there. It seemed they could do little but run him off. Sophie watched him sprint away as Riordan emerged.

'Can you have someone come as a messenger to the house? I have a package to send home and I want Halestrap to think I'm sending whatever it is he is looking for. Make sure there are men at Rowengate to see who it is who is spying and catch him. I'll go out tomorrow, somehow, so I hope Halestrap will follow me. He can stay hidden better here in Town, but at home there are few others about. It should be easy to see who else is interested,' she said quickly.

His eyes widened as they helped Mariah

to her feet. 'Of course, miss.' He said a few pleasantries about how sorry he was that the other fellow was such an uncivil beast before he took his leave.

Sophie linked her arm in Mariah's. 'Are you truly not hurt?'

'My pride is hurt more than anything I believe. Sophie, we really have to find a way to stop that awful man. I can't imagine how you can even leave the house knowing he is lurking.'

Sometimes she wondered as well. 'Well, I'm hoping this little plan will catch some-one else and then we can get Jasper home again in his own bed. Halestrap's capture can only be a matter of time. I hope. He can't be very well either.' They walked for several minutes, quiet, passing on their route the warehouse where Tilly now worked. The reason for her dismissal was still a mystery.

'Mariah, is there a reason that your aunt let Tilly go?'

'Nothing against poor Tilly, I assure you, or any of the rest. She said there had been a turn in her finances. Letting go those in the house who had been with her longest, meant she could hire new people for half of what she was paying for experience. She paid none of them before she put them out.

I am ashamed to be related to her because of it.'

Deep in her heart Sophie could feel the answer to the question even before she asked it. 'She wouldn't have a thousand pounds to give away, would she?'

'In a bet perhaps, but as a kind gesture I doubt it.' Mariah looked at her for a moment. 'Did she offer you such an amount?'

'One day, just after we arrived, she called it a nest egg in case she didn't find me a husband. She said she would put it in the bank that afternoon, I thought of it the other day and realized that was the last I heard of the money.'

'Oh, Sophie, I am so sorry, I never thought she would bring you into such things.'

Mariah started to laugh. 'Does it make me a bad person to say that I'm overjoyed the house is in uproar since she let them go? Her old servants knew all her likes and dislikes; life ran faultlessly. Now, she can't even get her breakfast to her liking. Her day goes downhill from there.'

Improper as it was, Sophie couldn't help but laugh as well. It was almost enough retribution for her having such horrid manners.

'Mariah?'

'I know that tone, Sophie, what idea have you?'

'Well it's only that Glensheen . . . Mr Fraser said it might be nothing more than a ramshackle place; he doesn't know.'

'Tilly, you mean? Someone to get things in order . . . does she even want to leave London? What if she has family here?'

Sophie shrugged her shoulders, not having thought through such things. 'It was only an idea.'

'I will certainly ask. I don't know if I have the skill to bring a place back to being habitable if it is truly bad. If I knew someone who could do it, or would be a godsend. I have never run a house before.'

'Would you care for some marzipan, Mariah? Help you get over your fright?'

There was the sparkle in her cousin's eyes. 'Why, I would love some.'

CHAPTER ELEVEN

Sophie had not been to a masked ball before. Not many were held and as her first season had been abruptly curtailed, there had been little time to attend one then. For once, she enjoyed herself. Being masked gave Sophie the opportunity to dance every dance. Even more, because her and Mariah's dresses matched, men she had already danced with asked again, thinking she was the other.

Mariah and Mr Fraser were dancing without Lady Sandbourne's knowledge. Sophie assumed they were setting plans in place whenever they were close enough to talk. They could parade about in the crush, no one knowing who anyone was.

'May I have the next two, miss?'

The man standing before her was tall and skinny, that's all she was aware of, but she took his hand readily. With the large number of couples, two sets were going at once and even then, the wait for turns was long. Sophie turned her thoughts to the puzzle of Greyfriars since her partner seemed to be shy once the original request had been made. Several times, she had asked if anyone knew of a crest, name, or anything that might advance her knowledge. It was always the same answer though. Until Jasper had his mind again, unravelling the puzzle was the only option.

'It is possible I could take her off your hands even with her trouble,' Sophie heard someone saying. Only when she recognized Lady Sandbourne's false simper did Sophie peer around to the other line of dancers. She could only see the back of Lady Sandbourne's head, but Lord Wolfenway grinned like a cat as he faced her direction. That set of teeth had been bared at her enough in the last weeks, she could never mistake their owner, mask or not. 'But I get half of the money you'll make on your wagers on the outcome of your little venture.'

'Agreed.'

Sophie tried not to scream. Mariah needed no help finding a husband, hiding Mr Fraser or not; Lady Sandbourne meant him for Sophie after all. The dance barely finished, she rushed past the dancers out into the night. How dare Lady Sandbourne use her fall in situation to bet that she could marry her off? Out past the carriages she went, letting the night swallow her up.

A stench caught her nose; a horse, perhaps — no. Her heart fell as she realized just what an idiot she had been. Her anger had got the better of her and her last bit of sense had fled. Just as Sophie turned to go back into the house, Halestrap jumped from behind a tree. Grabbing hold of her tight, there was no chance she would break his grasp this time. Fetid breath filled her nose.

'Where's Greyfriars?'

Mr Kittridge's words flooded back into her head. *They only have to get their hands on him.* Sophie did the only thing she could.

'George!' she shouted at the top of her lungs. Halestrap was pulling her further away from the house when, God, two men came from out of nowhere.

'She has the treasure!' Halestrap yelled, trying to get away. The men had hold of him, but, in an instant, he was free again. He rushed at her, seeing nothing but treasure, hurting her in the process was immaterial. He had a hand on her again; this time she saw the knife coming at her just before he was tackled. One of them yelled and more men came running. Six, no, eight. Dear Lord, how much had Mr Kittridge spent to see to her in safety?

Halestrap stared at her with crazed eyes that scared her even as four men held him flat to the ground. He fought like a man possessed. If there had been any less of them, he would have surely broken free. Another kept a pistol aimed at him.

'She knows where to find it! Make her tell me where it is and you can have half!'

Sophie was knocked off balance, but she didn't care that no one was there to help her rise. 'I don't know where anything is,' Sophie protested. She sat there feeling the weight lift off her chest at the sight of him held down. 'For the last time, I don't know who Greyfriars is! I have never known. I could have told you that without your strangling me.' Finally, a hand reached down to help her up. She stood eye to eye with Mr Fraser. Mariah was with him looking very worried.

'Are you all right?' Her cousin asked quietly.

George interrupted though. 'Your plan worked, miss. The riders just made it back with a letter a few hours ago. He'd sent word you were to be here so here we are. Might have saved you this if the grounds weren't so large. You've got a good set of lungs on you,' he finished with a smile.

'Who sent word?'

'Your father hired a gardener shortly after you came to London. He wasn't very good at his duties, but spied well.'

While eight men took Private Halestrap to army headquarters, two more still stood by her side making sure there was no one else.

'Go, and marry Mr Fraser. You need not worry about me staying here. I'll go to Phillippa, and then home. My place isn't here.'

'Sophie, what happened? Why did you leave the ball in such a hurry?'

'Your aunt has wagered she can marry me off against odds that no one would have me. I heard Lord Wolfenway say he would take me off her hands for half the proceeds. I hate to think how much she has wagered.'

Mariah looked back at the house as if hit in the stomach. 'She wouldn't . . . dear Lord, Sophie, I'm sorry.'

'You knew?' Sophie cried.

'Of the bet? Heaven forbid, you think me that cruel? It's the family secret that she gambles worse than any rake there is. I said as much that she needed money when I told you of her offer. She had to sell her barouche last winter. We should have had none if not for yours.'

'I mentioned that to her and she said you must have given the wrong impression, that it was only to save my parents' feelings. She even gave me a thousand pounds, in case I didn't marry, to visit you without needing charity.'

Mariah laughed faintly. 'Lud! She'd never admit it to anyone. Mama warned me when the offer came that she used girls each season to throw herself in the path of rich or titled men. She means marriage, which is all that can save her finances now, but it always seems to end in more gambling. I suggested you come so I'd have someone to talk to if she left me to my own devices. The two of us could keep watch for the other. Betting on a person, though, is a new low for her.'

Mr Fraser was staring behind Sophie, as if keeping watch. 'I'll need a week to clear up business here in Town. Perhaps you can busy yourselves in the shops buying Mariah's wedding clothes and stay out of Lady Sandbourne's grasp. Sophie, you're more than welcome to accompany us to Scotland.'

'On your honeymoon?' She laughed. 'No, I promised Mrs Beresford that I would visit when I left London. If I am welcome, I would gladly come in perhaps a month.'

'Lady Sandbourne is at the door ready to come out.' Mr Fraser whispered.

So he was keeping watch. 'Go around and

find the side door I saw. Alone, I cause no scandal, but if she finds you two. . . .'

Was it truly over? Need she worry? Her eyes half closed as she let her anxiety slip away. Jasper was alive and more a thief in his own mind than he was in actual particulars. He was healing slowly. Private Halestrap was captured. Now, if only she could keep Lady Sandbourne from collecting on her wagers. . . . Somehow, that had become a priority, for the principle of the matter. Was she willing to endure the rest of her life with her mother though, to see it done? That was the real question she pondered. Jasper's treasure no longer mattered.

'I heard there was a commotion outside at the ball last night,' Lady Sandbourne said, as Sophie was just about to raise a fork to her mouth at breakfast. The cook always laid out a substantial meal of eggs, bacon, breads, and such after a ball; the exertion certainly brought out their hunger the next morning.

Her fork lowered slowly. 'Yes, my lady, they caught the man who attacked me.'

'Thank heavens!' Mariah cried. 'I've been so worried.'

She should have been an actress, Sophie thought to herself. 'He used to serve with my brother and they believe the fighting touched his head. He's a deserter, so the army has him now.'

'Then you don't need these silly men to guard you anymore,' Lady Sandbourne said casually, as she put a delicate forkful in her mouth.

'Probably not, but those silly men are the ones who caught him. He would still be out there waiting for me if not for them.'

Lady Sandbourne sniffed just loudly enough for Sophie to hear it. 'Well, yes, of course. I didn't mean otherwise. I just tire of knowing I am being followed.'

'You weren't being followed,' Sophie said under her breath.

'Now then, we have to see Princess d'Alembert this morning. I hear she is short of money. I wonder if she will have the nerve to ask me,' Lady Sandbourne announced, unhearing of the comment.

Sophie swallowed hard hoping she could pull this off. 'Mariah and I had wondered if perhaps we could go shopping this morning. You can visit the princess and we can bring back news of any new fashions when we return.'

'Oh, yes. Please, Aunt Sandbourne. I do so need a new bonnet for the dress Inviolata has just finished,' Mariah added quickly.

'And gloves for my new ball gown. Ribbons of course.' Sophie kicked her under the table, but Mariah kept mentioning things she needed regardless.

'Very well,' Lady Sandbourne agreed after about the fifth thing Mariah pleaded she needed.

Then, one morning, they woke early and dressed in their riding clothes before heading to the park for a ride. In the park waited the barouche which had been packed with their things, including all the dresses Sophie had acquired. She considered it ample payment for using her as a wager.

Mariah was married in a lavish ceremony in her village church before leaving for her honeymoon to Scotland as Mrs Fraser. It was done before a letter arrived at the Randolphs' home claiming that:

Mariah has undoubtedly eloped off to Scotland with an unsuitable young man named Fraser. A duke was asking after her and was most upset that she was gone from his company. Please Brother, could you join me in the search? It is entirely my fault for not watching her better. I placed her in the clutches of the man in the first place; I should know my acquaintances better, but I believed Lady Naismith was always a solid woman.

Sophie was in her barouche heading for Cornwall with a fond hug of goodbye when the letter arrived. Mariah had been gone more than a week before it was deemed worthy of her parents' notice.

Staring at the turn in the road which led to Cornwall, Sophie realized her mistake. She hadn't much of the money left that her father had given her after buying clothes and such, paying Tilly, and her first trip to Cornwall.

'Go to Coverly Court instead.'

'But your brother?' Riordan argued.

'When I could gallivant about with fifty pounds, I forgot the economy of the last two years. I'm returned to real life, George. I've only five pounds, and I have to see you get back to London once you've driven me there. I cannot go to Cornwall until I have some funds from the bank. We can be at Coverly before nightfall.'

He was already shaking his head. 'William will reimburse anything it takes to get you to Cornwall. You needn't pay for my return.'

'Mr Kittridge is a friend; he is not my reticule to dip into any time I need money.

At last I can send the letter that it is safe for Jasper to return home. Anjanette will get him back when he is well enough. He's still lying there asleep, the last I heard, so my hovering over him worrying won't help. He has Anjanette already sitting vigil. I can pray here as well as there.'

Riordan groaned a bit, but eventually turned the barouche towards the direction of Coverly Court.

'Sophie, whatever are you doing here?' Phillippa exclaimed, as Sophie was announced. 'Don't tell me the rumours are actually true? Everard went to Town this week on business and heard some just dreadful gossip.'

Sophie sank into the chair next to her friend. 'If you mean that Lady Sandbourne wagered she could marry me off when the odds were against her, then, yes, it is true. And she paraded my trouble to an entire dinner party because she wanted some entertainment, yes, as well. However, on a better note, they have caught the man who was attacking me.'

'And Mariah eloping to Scotland?'

Sophie laughed at that and related the tale to her friend.

Phillippa was laughing. 'Then you are here

for a long visit?'

'If you'll have me. Mariah has asked that I visit her in Scotland in a month. I don't think I can bear going home just yet.'

'Of course, you're as welcome as my own family. Everard is to be in London for some weeks on business. He's seeing to the sale of the London house and the purchase of the new one. The gossip was all relayed by letter. I am already bored, and he has only been gone a week.' Phillippa watched her for a moment. 'You haven't any idea as to why she placed the bet in the first place?'

'She's a bored, wealthy woman without a husband. I heard that she has had a girl to stay with her every season and has always triumphed in marrying them off quickly. My guess is that it lost its challenge.'

'Everard heard at his club how much was bet against it by all the various participants. Do you care to hear?'

'Why not? It can be my final shame.'

'Fifty thousand pounds is tied up in it, all told. Lady Sandbourne herself bet a thousand, but if she wins, it will bring her fifty.'

'I thought it had to be a large sum since the man she was trying to tempt said he would do it for half the proceeds. But that wouldn't explain why she kept perfectly respectable men away. Tradesman or not, it would have been fifty thousand pounds for her.' Sophie closed her eyes just wishing she hadn't gone back to London. The only good to come of it was finding Phillippa again.

Every morning Sophie woke and played Mozart, a small payment for her keep. She didn't see Phillippa most mornings but she played just the same. Days had passed before she felt Phillippa's hand rest on her shoulder as it once had, and she sat down next to her on the bench.

'I don't want to go home,' Sophie whispered. It was the first time she had admitted it aloud. She might have said she couldn't bear the thought of returning, but to come right out and say it, was a shock.

'You're welcome in our home as long as you have need of it, Sophie.'

'I was Mariah's companion and look where it ended, the laughing stock of Town again and not my own fault.'

'Sophie, not one acquaintance showed interest? I find that hard to believe.'

'I know not if he was interested, but there is one I should say I liked. He, at least, never held my family against me.'

'Who might that be?'

'Mr Kittridge of course, but I am sure I shan't see him again.'

'Intriguing.'

With Phillippa ill for much of the mornings, it left Sophie to wander the gardens alone, and more importantly, now without fear of attack. The woods all around Coverly Court became well known as she explored. The village, too.

'Pardon me, miss,' a man said, after he bumped into her as she looked at ribbons yet again. She wanted nothing, but it had become a habit to look and see if there was anything new. 'Why, Miss Greenwood, whatever are you doing here?' he said, before she had a chance to turn around.

Spinning quickly at her name, she found Mr Asquith, the elder. Had he not heard the news? 'I am visiting friends in the neighbourhood.'

'But I thought everyone was in London. The National Gallery is open, all the young ladies have gone to Town for the masters.'

'I went for the masters several years ago, Mr Asquith. I prefer to visit a dear friend who cannot stay in London.'

'I thought I heard you had become engaged —'

'You must have mistaken me for another. I am not engaged to anyone,' Sophie interrupted, before he could say a name. She didn't really care with whom the gossips linked her: she would not return to London.

'My sons, you know, were quite enamoured of you that evening. If you should come to Town, I would invite you to dinner. Perhaps we could get you engaged after all.'

Sophie forced herself not to roll her eyes. 'I really am at the disposal of my friend. I cannot abandon her to her sickbed alone without her husband to comfort her as he will be away for some weeks. I've an invitation to travel to Scotland after that. I should be in time for the pheasant shooting. My cousin has just married and her husband has an estate there. I dare say I shan't come back to Town this season.'

'Oh, they will be disappointed to hear that.' A man outside called to him and he bade his goodbyes. With one last look at the merchandise available, Sophie found nothing new since the day before and followed Mr Asquith only moments later. A voice stopped her cold, his voice . . . she would have delighted at hearing Mr Kittridge again, but no, this was Lord Wolfenway.

'I'm not going to kidnap the girl to get her back to London for some wager I have no part in,' Mr Asquith replied.

'No part!' Wolfenway gasped. 'You have ten thousand pounds that she will marry, one of the few that do.'

'Only after I had dinner with her and saw her with that Kittridge fellow. There was a match there if I ever saw one.'

'What do I care about him? The wager was a *titled* man, not some tradesman. It's twenty-five thousand pounds if she marries me.'

'I only bet *any* marriage, so it doesn't matter to me who as long as she marries.'

Well, now she knew why men in trade had been kept away from her. Sophie closed her eyes hoping she wouldn't see Lady Sandbourne ever again. Hoping, because she might very well throttle her if she ever got close enough. She walked around the corner to confront them and both men turned a peculiarly bright shade of red.

'I should ask the lady before you make plans as to how to spend your fortune. Kidnap *is* the only chance you have at the match, for you are terribly bad at being overheard — now, and on the night of the ball.'

Wolfenway started sputtering and Sophie walked off, back to the woods around Coverly Court, before either man found his tongue. No one she knew would be there. She could live out the infamy alone.

CHAPTER TWELVE

Mr Beresford folded the letter from Phillippa with a smile, which grew broader when, not a few minutes later, Mr Kittridge entered for their meeting. He had returned to Town only the day before.

'Kittridge, my good man, how would you like to do a service for a very deserving woman?'

Mr Kittridge groaned. 'If you mean Miss Asquith, I danced with her at the Chancellors'. Wasn't that enough? She stepped on my toes so often, they're still sore.'

Mr Beresford's smile widened. 'I know why Miss Greenwood has left Town and I know where she is currently.'

Kittridge laughed faintly. 'She's gone to Coverly Court then. Missing your wife?'

'Haven't you heard about the wager placed upon her?'

Kittridge raised his eyes from the papers in his hand. 'What wager?'

'Lady Sandbourne wagered she would marry Miss Greenwood to a man of title by the end of the season. Bad enough, but if she won, she'd receive a full fifty thousand pounds. Lord, even your Mr Asquith is one of those betting.'

Kittridge's smile soon matched his. 'How would you like to accompany me to dinner this evening?'

'Ready to call out the marchioness, are you?'

Kittridge's laugh filled the club. Other members shushed him quickly. 'Lady Sandbourne is to be there this evening, and you and I are the only ones who know where Miss Greenwood is. Shall we ruin her evening by letting the news slip that there will be no marriage to a man of title?'

'I'm glad you said a man of *title*. My dear wife had another piece of news. I was to persuade you to visit Coverly. Miss Greenwood misses you.'

'The woman is wrenching fifty thousand pounds from a marchioness and she misses me. That doesn't sound like the Miss Greenwood I know.'

Beresford handed over the letter. 'The first half is rather personal, but the second half pertains to you.'

Sophie knows I am a bored mother-to-be and so hopeless she answered my question of whether she had any inclination to anyone while she was in Town. 'I know not if he was interested, but there is one I should say I liked.' When I asked who, she answered, 'Mr Kittridge, but I am sure I shan't see him again.' Everard, do persuade him to come and visit. She seems so melancholy, especially after running into Asquith and Wolfenway in the village. Can you imagine, they pretended to run into her and convince her to return to London? Just so they could have their sport with this whole wager business. Sophie's not some filly to bet upon in a race.

Kittridge lifted his head. 'Is the woman dense?'

'My wife? As she said, she's a bored mother-to-be.' Beresford looked at him for a moment. 'Not my wife. Were you that obvious?'

'I would have thought so. I don't kiss every woman I meet. It would seem the lady has been so humiliated, she cannot believe it to be more than a flirtation.'

'Dinner tonight, you say? I think I can join you.' The footman brought them brandy as

Kittridge scratched his jaw in thought.

'Read the rest of the letter — the other side.'

Kittridge narrowed his eyes as he turned it over. 'No, not the cousin as well?'

'Lady Sandbourne still thinks she eloped. Hasn't a clue Mariah married with her father's permission.'

Kittridge started to laugh. 'Oh, I am not a nice man, not with what is going through my head.'

'Tell me it's fitting and I'll be as much an accomplice as you need.'

'Undoubtedly.'

The outside of the house they pulled up to was imposing, even for Mayfair. 'Who is the host? I suppose I should know,' Beresford asked, as they ascended the stairs to the front door.

'Princess d'Alembert.'

Beresford stopped short. 'You never mentioned a princess. How were you invited again?' he asked under his breath.

'She lived for a time in Jamaica with a relation when the Revolution was at its height. She lost everything. Any family she had with money was put to the guillotine. The princess is a little short of funds at the moment. I have decided she'll win what she needs in a wager.'

Beresford looked at his companion, realizing that while he might be in trade and laugh at being new to society, there was nothing tradelike about him. 'You know her well enough for her to ask for money?'

'She's the first girl I kissed when I was all but fourteen, but, no, she'd never ask. She married her husband while she lived in Jamaica and has a habit of gambling away his yearly income. It's rather common knowledge in fact. He's not here tonight, therefore she can have her winnings tucked away before he ever learns of it.'

'Remind me never to anger you, Kittridge. I think you see justice in a completely different way than I.'

Kittridge smiled widely as they were admitted. 'My father put me aboard one of our ships at the age of fifteen to see we weren't cheated when we sold our rum. I took over the land side of the operation for more than a decade, before he died. He also taught me to respect women, especially one who takes on a scheming marchioness and denies her fifty thousand pounds.'

They were separated at the table for dinner, Kittridge sitting next to a duke. Coffee was served later when everyone was in the drawing-room together. A card table had been set up, but he ignored it, circulating amongst the guests, carrying a small book. He caught Lady Sandbourne's eye several times, but he was on the opposite side of the room and wasn't going to indulge her curiosity just yet. It amused Kittridge to note that Lady Sandbourne had dressed to allow her to be best displayed against the red silk walls and coffered cherry-wood ceiling.

'Mr Kittridge, I demand my part in your entertainment.'

He tried not to smile. *Now* he was good enough for her to speak to. 'I'm taking wagers, Lady Sandbourne.'

'Oh, I do love a good wager. What are you betting on?'

Kittridge turned slowly and levelled his eyes at her. 'I'm taking bets as to how long it was before you knew Miss Mariah Randolph had married with your brother's permission in her village church. Beresford, over there, is taking bets on how many men you ran off in keeping Miss Greenwood from marrying a man in trade so that you could win your bet. Oh, and his grace near you is taking bets as to how many know you haven't a farthing to your name. Gambling is such a nasty habit.' Sitting next to a duke had obviously produced some additional gossip and another who wanted to see the woman brought to task.

Lady Sandbourne stumbled back, white as a sheet, the crash as she upset the coffee tray echoed in the silent room. No one said a thing, as she lay there sprawled on the floor.

Kittridge pulled out guineas from his pocket and started counting them out to Princess d'Alembert. 'Don't smile, or they might notice I hadn't got to you yet,' he muttered under his breath.

'Thank you, William.'

'What is that for?' Lady Sandbourne gasped, as she attempted to pick herself up from the floor.

'Can't you guess? The princess deduced you would find out when I told you of Miss Randolph's marriage to Mr Fraser. Did you really not know? It is a bad bet on my part; she had the advantage. But I do love a good wager.'

'I'm a marchioness,' Lady Sandbourne gurgled quietly, but no one came to her aid.

'I've never taken a wager on a person before, but after you set such a precedent, I saw no reason not to bet on others as well. Beresford, take the last of the wagers on how many men she ran off and we can get the answer from Lady Sandbourne herself. We'd be here all night trying to discern it ourselves.'

'Sophie ran off with you, didn't she? You're just here to get your share of the wager,' Lady Sandbourne hissed.

Kittridge stared at her. 'I don't have a title, madam, so how could I win? I believe she went away to escape your scheming. But, we people in trade need our entertainments too.' Lady Sandbourne's eyes opened wide as Kittridge came closer. 'Perhaps, my lady, I don't appreciate being thought beneath the touch of the woman who's denied you fifty thousand pounds. After your appalling display of bad manners, I'd marry her for no other reason than it would deny you such a sum.'

Lady Sandbourne snorted as she finally regained her footing. 'You're the one betting against me. Obviously you need the money,' she accused.

In the corner, Rhys Dyson choked on his brandy. 'Man bought Falwood, the old Duke of Delisle's estate that the Crown had taken over because there was no heir; he owns the largest rum distillery in the Caribbean with the Royal Navy contract of some one hundred thousand pounds a year, and just bought Beresford's London house,' he got out between coughs. 'When I need a loan, I don't go to the Bank of England. I visit William Kittridge and his father before him.'

The noise of a side table toppling over rang out again as Lady Sandbourne put her weight on it trying not to falter again. Mr Kittridge had already left by the time everyone turned at the news of his wealth, a fact he never flaunted. In his absence, their whispers turned to Lady Sandbourne for a topic. With heads together and all eyes upon her, she fled.

CHAPTER THIRTEEN

Some days later, Sophie was lying in the thick grass outside Coverly half-asleep when she heard someone approaching. Phillippa was coming into the clearing.

'Feeling better then?'

'So far; it pains me to have been such a dismal hostess for three whole weeks so I thought I would join you. Petry will be coming soon with a picnic,' Phillippa answered, sitting down on the grass nearby.

'Delightful, but you aren't being a dismal hostess. I wouldn't dream of you keeping me entertained while neglecting your own health.'

'Today I've had a very good day so far. I received a letter from Everard, or I should have been out to join you earlier. Lady Sandbourne is being taken to court. She's almost a hundred thousand pounds in debt. There's some duke involved and he's quite determined to see that he gets every pound he's owed.' Suddenly Phillippa changed the subject. 'If I stay well this afternoon, shall we have dinner at the inn in the village, as we did when we were young and our fathers let us feel like grown ups?'

'And then sent Jasper to watch over us like little girls.' Sophie smiled at the memory. 'I rather thought you and Jasper would marry. I always liked the idea of you as my sister.'

'How would it be if *I* watch over you now as Jasper can't do it?' Sophie felt her heart beat faster as she realized it was Mr Kittridge's voice. This time it was no fantasy, she would know his voice anywhere.

'What brings you to Coverly, Mr Kittridge? This is an unexpected surprise,' Phillippa said quickly, trying to rise to her feet.

'No, please, stay seated,' he protested, and was on the ground next to Sophie soon enough. 'When Petry admitted me, he told me of the picnic and is adding more food. I hope I'm not intruding.'

'Of course not. We were just remembering the old days with Greyfriars,' Phillippa announced.

'The what?' Sophie and Mr Kittridge gasped at once.

'Am I remembering it wrong? Isn't that what we used to call Jasper when he crept around watching over us? He used to wear that old grey coat of your father's; it made him look like a monk.'

'Mr Kittridge, I'm going to need you to kill someone for me,' Sophie hissed.

He was laughing when he asked who, but it died quickly enough when he saw the look in her eyes.

'Jasper and my father. It's been at home all this time. I was attacked because Jasper wrote that letter when whatever it was, was already with Father. It wasn't Greyfriars, it was the Grey Monk. That's what we called Papa's coat when we were children. No wonder I didn't recognize the name. Jasper sent something to Papa explaining this shadowy stuff and said Greyfriars, not Grey Monk. I doubt Papa ever knew the name we gave it either. Papa thought Jasper was getting into spying, or some such nonsense, but he was really telling him to keep it safe. Everyone just assumed it was a man, any man but our father. I demand you kill him for me.'

'And your father didn't make any mention of having received any treasure?' Mr Kittridge asked.

'But he did.' Sophie remembered everything of the conversation she had had with him before she left for London. 'The night

Mariah came with the invitation to London, Papa gave me fifty pounds; he said Jasper had sent it to him to buy some luxury — brandy and cigars, but Papa couldn't do it when the rest of us had so little. Maybe it wasn't worth as much as Jasper thought, or Papa put it away to increase the sum we live on each year. Maybe Papa knew enough that it was stolen and he wasn't going to appear to have lots of money and have to explain how he got it. I don't know. I just know that Jasper put me in the middle of it for no purpose.'

'Stolen? Sophie, what on earth are you talking about?' Phillippa demanded, and Sophie explained the whole sordid mess.

'If you had only confided in me, Sophie. I thought he was looking for Jasper when he shouted in the coach that day we left London, but you didn't mention it again. I thought you knew what it was about.'

'I didn't learn he wasn't a thief until weeks later when I spoke to someone in his regiment. When I was here, it was in dread that it would be shown that Jasper was a thief, and I refused to drag anyone else down in the scandal. Even his superiors called it spoils of war. It was all his own sense of honour that made him call himself a thief.'

'You trusted Mr Kittridge and not me,

your oldest friend? I am truly hurt.'

Mr Kittridge's laugh made Sophie's stomach churn. Why had she ever told Phillippa she had liked him? Now she would read all sorts of things into it if she even blushed.

'Trust me, Mrs Beresford, she would rather I had not known. I only found out when she left her letter in my lap and grabbed my handkerchief by mistake.'

'You didn't say what brings you here again,' Sophie said, trying to turn the conversation.

'Mr Beresford told me of you being here, Miss Greenwood.'

Sophie felt the blush coming to her cheeks as he smiled at her.

'How shocking you are, Mr Kittridge,' Phillippa laughed as Petry approached with the picnic.

'If you please, madam, Miss Windom is at the door. We've been offering her some food to take home to her mother, but she refuses to take it. The girl is positively gaunt. I don't worry often but this time I do. Could you please come and see she takes as much as you can make her?'

'Oh, yes, of course. I'll be back in time to eat. Do carry on, Petry, and lay it out. Forgive me, Sophie. Ever since our neighbour died, his wife and daughter have been living on pennies, they hate to take charity. Now the mother is ill too.'

'Perhaps they would be less opposed to taking help if you offered Miss Windom the position of companion with a stipend. You are going to have a child soon. It wouldn't be like being a maid when she knows you have a full staff,' Sophie suggested.

'Sophie, I could kiss you.' Phillippa rushed off.

Petry threw out a red tartan tablecloth and started setting out dishes in a shady spot on the other side of the clearing. It looked like a wine roasted gammon, chicken, and some gingerbread cakes and even some vegetables from the hothouse.

'You know that's not a half bad idea. I could kiss you myself.'

Sophie shook her head. 'Mr Kittridge, whatever shall I do with you? Petry will think —'

'Let me compliment you as often as possible and leave no doubt in his mind then. If he is going to tell tales, I would prefer he tells them about true actions.'

'After the season I have had, I'm afraid I am too jaded for idle flattery.'

'Idle? I would never compliment idly. Does that mean you give me leave to compliment you as I wish as long as it doesn't lead to offers of *carte blanche?*'

'Gladly. You would live up to Lady Sandbourne's ill thoughts of you if you did so. I should hate to see her right.' She added an afterthought. 'I shouldn't be alone with you like this.'

'Shouldn't, or don't want to?'

Sophie closed her eyes. 'Shouldn't.' She finally admitted.

'Then I still have hope?'

'Why do you talk so?'

'Are you saying you like me and I don't have to wonder?'

Sophie opened her eyes to find Mr Kittridge very close, so close the bay rum filled her nose as the blue of his eyes sparkled in the sunlight. Softly his hand ran along her cheek.

'Say you do not like me and I shall never mention it again and even stop my compliments, as much as you deserve them.'

For the first time in her life, Sophie's heart stopped in her chest. Two years ago, it had been heartbreak, now it stopped dead with fear. 'I should say so but I cannot.'

'Then why do you keep saying I shouldn't say what I do? Are you worried you wouldn't have an adequate living?'

'Money?' She half laughed even as she realized his words held more than gentle flirting. Surely, he wasn't implying marriage? 'You think I worry about a man's money? I've been digging my own garden for two years. On one thousand pounds, and only two of us, I could live like a queen. I'm certain you have more than that. Don't you dare bring up a title either.'

'Then why did you readily accept my teasing before and now sound so missish. I like to see you spar with words.'

Why indeed? It was hard to think though with his thumb caressing her cheek. Her mother's voice rang in her head and she knew the reason well enough. 'I cannot bear to go back home and yet I could not bear a match where a man would see me as my father does my mother. I don't think my father would even give his permission if he suspected it would turn out such. I suppose I sound missish when the worry of that surfaces.'

'I cannot see you ending up as a shrew to be hated, nor can I see you not following your own judgement and entering such a match.'

'Why did you truly come?'

'Truthfully? I consider it an insult to my honour that you left me to endure all those women throwing themselves at me without you being there to fend them off.'

'Do you wish to call me out? Pistols at dawn and all that? I'm surprised no one has suggested it already with all the goings on I've had this season.'

'Because of gossip, there's only one solution then: you'll just have to agree to marry me before you know how much I'm worth.'

'Don't tease.'

'Trust me, I whould not tease about an offer of marriage. This is fine thanks I get, too, when you won't even give me an answer, just chide me for joking.'

Sophie was still hardly able to believe her ears. 'How am I supposed to act? You go from flirting to offers of marriage all within an hour. How do I know you aren't funning?' That did it, the smile that had lodged him in her dreams before she even knew his name, returned.

'I haven't a title. You can say yes without Lady Sandbourne winning her wager.'

'No, but Mr Asquith will win his wager. He placed his own wager that I would; I overheard him say so when he saw us together.' As much as she protested, refusal of the idea of marriage was impossible now. Even her anger couldn't overcome the words that he had truly mentioned marriage.

'He's a very observant man then.'

'Why would you even ask me?' she whispered, all the time conscious Petry was undoubtedly watching the whole thing.

'A little privacy, Petry,' he called out, as if reading her mind, and Sophie heard the clatter of dishes stop. 'Open your eyes,' he whispered, so close to her ear she could feel his breath on her neck. The smell of bay rum surrounded her like a cloud as she opened her eyes. Not that he knew she did, his head was still bowed at her neck. Then she felt the heat of his mouth on her in a single kiss.

'Look at me,' Sophie ordered. With his blue eyes staring into hers, all he had to do was push a strand of hair behind her ear and she could hardly think straight.

'I will gladly marry you, dowry or not, whether that treasure of your brother's is fifty pounds or fifty thousand. I'm asking you now so that you know, I can't be interested in money. But I do it on one condition: you have to agree to spar with words the rest of your days. No more of this sounding missish.'

'I thought you came here to improve the family name. Marrying me won't do that.'

'No, I'm here because we've more money than we know what to do with. I decided property was the best option to keep it safe from drunken gamblers, harebrained schemes and extravagant wives. Thaddeus desires a wife with a title; *he* wishes to improve the family name. Me, I've found I rather love to hear of an impoverished baron's daughter who has denied a marchioness fifty thousand pounds on the principle of the thing and refused to marry a debt-ridden rake.'

Sophie lowered her eyes as her heart beat heavy in her chest. *Should she dare?* 'William.' He pulled his head back quickly at the use of his Christian name. 'The man I am engaged to may call me Sophie.' Mr Kittridge. . . . William, only smiled.

'You'll need a new wardrobe, I imagine,' Phillippa said from the edge of the clearing. 'Perhaps I could come to Town for a few short weeks and help out a friend.'

Sophie made a face. 'Oh lud, I will have to start wearing those dreadful little caps. I've never really liked those.'

'Small price to pay,' William teased.

'See, Sophie? I told you I'd help you to be a little mercenary if you set your eyes on our Mr Kittridge.'

'I didn't. . . . You told him I was here.' Sophie turned her eyes slowly to William, so close he could kiss her if he only moved a few inches. 'Just how much are you worth?

Phillippa wouldn't call it mercenary otherwise.'

'Regretting it already? For shame, Sophie.' Sophie opened her mouth to protest, then froze when he started to grin. 'In that case I'll make you wait until after the wedding before you know.'

Wedding? He actually said wedding. Sophie bit her lip.

'Could we elope, William? I should so like to have something to tell my children when I have become a settled matron. I am already expected in Scotland in a week's time.' In all truthfulness, if she had to give a reason, it was that she wanted her mother to have no part in this matter. If she had not been so greedy, Sophie would not have had bets made against her marrying at all.

'Whatever you wish.' The look in William's eyes was enough to make her blush alone.

They sat for hours in the clearing until Phillippa declared she was hungry again and feeling well enough to walk to the village. Sophie forgot about everything as they sat in the inn well into the night, savouring a beefsteak pudding and apple pie. Petry sent the carriage for them knowing Phillippa's state; she was worn out. William though suggested he and Sophie walk and suddenly she was alone with him on the road as the light faded.

'You were quiet at dinner,' he commented, as they left the last of the houses. 'Not regretting your decision I hope. I promise your one hundred pounds is settled on you.'

Sophie laughed. 'No. You will think me childish to mention my reason.' Her laugh died as William cupped her cheek in his hand.

'There was a reason I wished to walk.'

And he kissed her. Nothing like the boyish attempts of the neighbour boy when she was fifteen. She could feel his fingers slipping in her hair holding her close. Was it her breathing that grew fast or his?

'William . . .' Sophie finally got out and he pulled back slightly.

His only reply was a grin before they were joined again. William's hands roamed lower, grazing the bare skin above her gown's bodice. The gasp she heard was not her own even though she felt it leave her lips.

It was dark enough she couldn't see the face in the carriage as they pulled apart, and she hoped that meant no one could see hers either.

'Sir, have your bit of muslin in private. Decent folk. . . .' A woman screeched.

Another voice interrupted, one she recognized. 'The directions to Coverly Court, sir, if you please.'

Sophie buried her face in his shoulder. 'Dear God, it's my parents,' she muttered. Sophie felt William shaking with laughter, but it wasn't *his* parents come to condemn after he quit London in all but disgrace. What right did he have to laugh at her predicament?

'Go; if you run, you can be there while I'm giving directions,' he whispered, before having the audacity to pat her on the backside in dismissal. She heard her mother gasp. 'Get your things packed to leave first thing in the morning. You wanted to elope. There will be no chance if they find out we are engaged. Ask Phillippa to lie until we are gone. I'll collect you at dawn.'

'Having fun, aren't you?' Sophie hissed, just before she rushed off in the darkness.

Sophie threw open the door, making Phillippa jump. 'My parents are coming. They didn't recognize me in the dark.'

'You weren't . . . were you?'

'Heaven forbid, woman, but they caught us kissing. I should still like to elope though. Could you lie about our engagement? William will be here first thing in the morning. If I want any say in my own wedding, it is my only hope.'

Phillippa's smile grew. 'Gladly. Petry, bring some wine for Miss Greenwood. Her colour's rather high for having been sitting here with me.'

Only a few sips were taken before Lord and Lady Canmore were announced.

'Sophie, whatever are we going to do with you? Twice leaving London in disgrace and still unmarried,' Lady Canmore screeched.

'Papa,' Sophie said, loud enough it shocked her mother into quiet. 'How long ago did Jasper send you that package?'

'What?'

Her mother snapped, turning on her, 'We are talking to you, miss! You're the one running off without anyone knowing where you were for weeks. Helping poor Mariah elope with a highly unsuitable man and offending your host. How we'll ever get back in Lady Sandbourne's good graces is beyond me.'

'That is simple, we will not,' Sophie said quietly. It worked far more effectively than shouting. Her mother just stared.

'What do you mean we will not?' Lady Canmore said, her voice grating on Sophie's ear after having been away from it for so long.

'Mariah is not married to an unsuitable man. She was married in her village church to a man her father approved of. Lady Sandbourne deemed him unsuitable. And as for no one knowing where I was, I wished it that way.' Lady Canmore opened her mouth to protest; Sophie knew the look in her eyes. But her father pulled her mother back allowing Sophie to finish. 'I left London because Lady Sandbourne had wagered she would marry me to a peer by summer's end when all of London was wagering against her. She put off any perfectly suitable man because he wasn't a peer and the one peer she did find would have only taken me for half of her winnings. I couldn't walk outside alone without fear of attack because Jasper was addlebrained enough to write that letter you forwarded to me when he full well knew one of his men was watching him. I don't know what he told you, Papa, but the letter you passed on was Jasper informing me of the whole sordid mess. I was half strangled because this man from his regiment wanted to know where Grey-friars was. A gardener you took on was spying on the letters I sent so he could discern where I was. I haven't come home because I do not wish to see either of you at the moment.'

'There's gratitude for you.' Her mother sniffed.

'So that's what happened to Jackson; he vanished without warning a few weeks ago.' Lord Canmore looked at his wife for a moment. 'I suppose you think I should have told you, Sophie,' Her father added. 'Simply put, I didn't realize it would lead him to you. Certainly not that Greyfriars meant to do anything to put danger in your way.'

'You received something from your son and didn't mention it to any of us?' Lady Canmore gasped at Sophie's words.

'It wasn't a fortune. It's in the bank earning interest. We should just about clear a few thousand a year now with everything coming in. I took on a gardener to save your hands — a bad choice it seems, Sophie — and can do some little things to make life easier. By the time Violet and Lily are old enough, they will have decent dowries.'

'We have money again and you did not tell me,' Lady Canmore hissed.

'And that is just why I haven't told you. To right all the old wrongs, we cannot spend as we once did.'

'But if Sophie could have a dowry again, she could go back to London and find a husband.'

'I refuse to go back.'

With that, Sophie walked out.

■ ■ ■ ■

Despite her stomach churning Phillippa sat at breakfast with only a cup of chocolate before her.

'I suppose Sophie is still angry with us and we shan't see her all day?' Lady Canmore questioned, as she filled a plate with everything laid out on offer.

'I think she is rather upset, but that isn't why you won't see her today. Do you still play the pianoforte, Lady Canmore? I learned to love Mozart at Rowengate after all.'

'No, I haven't played in years.'

'Pity.' Phillippa sipped at her chocolate trying not to look at the heaped plate before Lady Canmore.

'Why won't we see her?' Lord Canmore asked eventually.

'She's on her way to Scotland.'

'Why ever is she going to Scotland?' Lady Canmore asked.

Phillippa noticed a slight gleam in Lord Canmore's eyes. *Did he know already?* 'Mariah's new husband has an estate there where they are honeymooning. The plan is to stop and marry on their way to see her. Sophie's fiancé was going for a special licence to save your interference in the match.'

Lady Canmore nearly spat her bacon across the table. 'What?'

'Oh yes. Mr Kittridge is a most delightful man. In rum and sugar, you know, just in from Jamaica.' Phillippa had a hard time keeping a straight face, but it was worth it to see Lady Canmore's expression.

'You must go after her, Benedick. She's throwing her life away.'

'Sit down and eat your breakfast,' Lord Canmore ordered. 'He saw me at my club in London and we settled her hundred pounds on her if she should accept him.'

'What sort of brigand would take her for a hundred pounds? Don't tell me she's with child and forced to marry him,' Lady Canmore shrieked.

'You read too many novels. Not every brigand cares what his wife has other than a pretty face and engaging manner, and we all know Sophie has both in excess. It's the penniless lords you have to watch out for. Not another word out of you. I will eat my breakfast in peace.'

Phillippa hid her smile in her cup of chocolate. If only Sophie knew what plotting there had been behind her back, she would kill her, no doubt about that, not even order Mr Kittridge to do it for her. Lord Canmore would tell his wife how much Sophie was worth in a few months and then forbid her to visit. That would be punishment enough for the anguish she had put Sophie through.

CHAPTER FOURTEEN

The church in the village nearest William's home in Somerset, was the most she had seen of anything. William had kept her away from the house, keeping his word that she shouldn't know his worth until after they were wed. She had seen a little of the village. There were several shops that were nicer than those she had access to at Rowengate. A port deep enough for large ships stood nearby with a quay loading. . . . Heavens!

'Riordan!' Sophie called and the man looked up. Phillippa, at her side, looked bemused that she should know the name of such an unkempt man.

'Miss, what brings you to see us?'

'A wedding.'

'How long till the boat is filled?' William asked, appearing behind them.

Riordan laughed. 'Would have been done several days ago, but you keep sending goods our way. You done now?'

'I am. Send the ship on its way and give everyone the day off tomorrow. They'll need to clean up though; I'm ordering them to the church.'

Riordan looked between the two of them for a quick moment before his eyes grew wide. 'Yours and William's?'

William smiled at Sophie, even if his words were for another. 'Mrs Beresford, you asked about planning the wedding breakfast, refusing to listen to any suggestions I might make, of course. The owner of the Hart and Hound has returned if you wish to speak to him.'

'Well, if you had eloped with me as I asked, she wouldn't feel she has to make it up to me.' Sophie replied sweetly.

William laughed, drawing the attention of most the men on the boats nearby. 'Must be all my fault.'

Riordan narrowed his eyes again. 'Seems a lot of trouble when you just have to tell cook and it will be done.'

William slipped Sophie's arm in his. 'Perhaps, Riordan, but she's yet to meet cook or even see the house. It's a surprise until after the wedding.'

Riordan opened his mouth, but William led them off before he could answer.

■ ■ ■ ■

The next morning was a blur. When Sophie woke, Phillippa helped her dress and they were taken to the church along a foggy lane. The church looked as old as England itself. Dark weathered stone stood hazy in the mist of early morning. Candles were lit within since the sun had not come out to illuminate the ancient stained glass. Somehow her own sisters stood there. Jasper. . . . Jasper stood there, pale, thin, but standing on his own. His arm tucked in Anjanette's, he looked in the other direction. So it was true. Sophie threw her arms around his neck and just held him.

'How ever did you get here?'

'Papa, dear girl. We got your letters weeks ago saying it was safe. Your fiancé went to Papa to ask for your hand. He knew you didn't want Mama here, but he wouldn't deny you the rest of us.'

'But I asked to elope.'

'Kittridge was certain he could persuade you here.'

That much was certain. 'How are you, Jasper, truly?'

'My shoulder still hurts a little, but it's healing. Also, it appears an angel hes been watching over me, and I just had to marry her.'

'Good.'

Then her father came to give her away.

'What did the two of you plan?' Sophie muttered.

'Nothing, child. I just saw you were well taken care of.'

'And how were you even certain I would say yes?'

'Because his eyes kept smiling even as I told him all the reasons why no man should ever consider you. No man looks like that if his affection is not returned. You used your season well.'

They beamed as she wed, they beamed as they ate a celebration breakfast, and they beamed as she rode off as Mrs William Kittridge. William himself drove the carriage, past the edge of town, the docks, before turning into the massive gates labelled Falwood where they rolled past open parkland with cascades, lakes and woodland walks. Sophie found herself in a medieval deer park, where immense red stags with antlers reaching higher than she stood ran off as the carriage disturbed them. The fog hid fields of green grass until they were upon them, each surrounded by woods hundreds of years old judging by the size of the oaks.

Here and there lakes and ponds broke the monotony of such verdant green.

'One thousand acres of park in case you were wondering.'

So large? Rowengate had only a few acres around the house itself. The rest was let to farmers paying rent. It had been that way even before their turn in fortune. 'Mr Kittridge, you'll spoil me.'

'Mr Kittridge? I don't even warrant a first name on our wedding day?'

Sophie felt her cheeks grow warm. Her wedding day! For two years it had seemed it would never happen. 'It's only been three days since we were engaged, not much time to get used to given names.'

'Then perhaps I'll forgive you.'

Sophie caught him smirking when she looked over. She was trying to think of a retort when they rounded a corner and, as if on cue, the fog cleared around the grounds revealing a house. There on a small rise a three-storey tower looking rather like castle battlements. It stood in another green expanse without a tree for protection. There was plenty of room to plant a garden just as she wished, and several trees to rest underneath someday. 'How beautiful, William. It's perfect.'

'You are truly content with so little?'

'I said once on the thousand pounds a year, and only two people, I could live like a queen. A cottage, a ship, a small manor, even a room in an inn. I shan't care what as long as I can call it my own.' William leaned near her ear and every nerve reminded her she had meant to speak to Phillippa about wedding nights.

'Now, I should remind you it's almost devoid of furniture. I'll need to ask you to fill it so I can do business, little though you think I do.'

All Sophie's mind could think of though was her lack of knowledge in all things marital. She could run a house, no doubt of that, no matter the finances. She could host parties without fail. . . . 'William, I've never. . . .' It seemed years since he had touched her and it was only days. As his fingers caressed her cheek Sophie knew her marriage would not be as her father's was with her mother.

'It impressed me greatly that you never asked questions, Sophie. Not how much I'm worth, not the size of the house. You just trusted it would be enough.'

Her laughter died at that and she looked back at the man that she now called husband. 'How much are you worth? Phillippa wouldn't call it mercenary.'

'I saw your father before I went to Coverly. I rather presumed you would say yes, so we drew up a marriage contract you just have to sign. You'll have a good sum if I die first, five thousand in pin money a year. I promised your one hundred pounds would always be yours, never fear.'

Sophie could only stare at him. His words gave her an odd feeling that the sum was suddenly far more than she wanted to think about. 'That didn't answer my question. How much are you worth?'

William smiled. 'Roughly six hundred thousand, that's after the purchase of the houses, but not including the property in Jamaica, or the contract with the government for our rum. I estimate we have thirty thousand a year.'

Sophie's knees felt weak and she was already sitting. And there was the man who kept smiling after all he knew about her.

'Your father is packing your things to send along so you may have them about you, oh, and he's forbidden your mother from visiting for a full year. That's his gift to you. I think perhaps we'll go to Jamaica for a visit . . . in a year's time.'

That in itself might have been the greatest gift he could give her. Money and houses — it was nice to know she would eat and not run barefoot through the streets, but William had been right. She trusted him to provide, and after the last two years, her expectations weren't extravagant. 'You would take me with you?'

'Of course.' He set the horses to a walk again. 'Now the entrance of the house is painted the blue of the seas of Jamaica, and I've said it matches your eyes so I'm putting my foot down and forbidding you to change it, but otherwise the house is certainly all yours to command.'

Sophie closed her eyes, and before she could even let the compliment sink in, gentle kisses brushed against her eyelids. Sophie felt him turning her head carefully. His deep lilting whisper floated to her ears. 'Open your eyes, Sophie.'

Her name more than anything surprised her, not some polite Miss Greenwood or more polite Mrs Kittridge. Slowly she lifted her lids, there some distance off was certainly no tower folly. The 600-year-old house never seemed to end — no, castle might have been a better word with its fortified towers, battlements and buttresses. Sophie was unable to control her laughter. The biggest house she had seen until then could fit into one wing of Falwood. Golden stone shone even in the mist that still remained and was reflected in the river that flowed past the edifice. Delightful flowering gardens, enclosed by a stone curtain wall surrounded it all.

At the sight of all that splendour her family struggled to the forefront of her mind. 'William, can we help my family a little, please?'

He sat back in the seat. 'I might have heard what price your father received for some captured French treasure. I don't think you have to worry about your family anymore.'

No, he couldn't have. 'You bought it and never told me?'

William shook his head slowly, looking rather surprised that she would think such a thing of him. 'Mr Dyson tried to give your father money after he heard from you about the fall in your fortunes, but your father would have none of it. He was amiable to the idea of selling goods though. It was no wonder Halestrap was determined, and your father received no more than its worth. A London jeweller set the value at fifty thousand pounds.' Then he started chuckling. 'I didn't know that the man Dyson was dealing with was your father until I went to ask for your hand. Dyson kept calling him Canmore.'

Sophie chuckled. 'See what you miss, hiding away with your pirated money? Any self-respecting gentleman would have at least learned the family name of a woman he was courting.'

'Any self-respecting lady of title would have realized a man was courting before he asked her to marry him.'

With a grin, Sophie gave him a most unladylike wink. 'Well, it seems I've forgotten to ask Mrs Beresford what to expect on my wedding night. I might be just as naïve when it comes to that as well.'

'I have a wedding gift for you. Then we'll make sure you aren't naïve when morning comes.'

She felt the blush stain her cheeks at the idea. He was truly going to spoil her if he kept this up. 'You've already done too much and I've given you nothing in return. I expected to elope, after all.'

'This gift cost me nothing. You needn't feel indebted over it. I just wanted to be the bearer of the news that Lady Sandbourne married the day I left London.'

'Isn't that good news? She'll be ecstatic.'

'Not when she's married to Viscount Wolfenway of Wolfenhame End. She's banished to Wales. She's penniless; your parents had more than she before Jasper's windfall.

She's let the estate and the house in London; she receives almost nothing from the farm rents.'

'She owed money to the duke, too,' Sophie murmured Tilly's words. It was fine satisfaction to know that such behaviour wasn't repaid with good tidings, but there was something else that really bothered her now. She was married to the man and she had no idea as to the answer. 'That is excellent news indeed, but there is one question I should like to ask without offending you.'

'You sound so mysterious. You may ask as long as it doesn't sound missish of course.'

'You aren't a smuggler, are you?'

His lip twitched for a moment and then the laughter started. 'What brought that to mind?'

Her colour turned even redder; the thought of him in her bed brought less embarrassment. 'The house where Jasper was staying . . . when I asked why they sent him there. I was told lace, silk —'

'Rum?' he finished for her. 'So, it was on a smuggler's ship they secreted him out of the country, to keep Halestrap from finding him.'

'You have such stories.' A finger over her mouth stopped her digging a bigger hole.

'You waited until after you were married

to me to ask such a question?'

Sophie opened her mouth, but she really didn't have an answer.

'Men like to hear such stories; I indeed have seen more than most, but I toss in some tales my father told me as well when I run dry and the wine is flowing. The only thing I've stolen in my life is a kiss or three.'

'There is one thing you've forgotten.'

'You call me thief?'

Sophie took a deep breath, 'You stole my heart, William. You don't think I'd marry any man dangling after me, do you?' Throwing his words back at him, he laughed silently as they rolled into the courtyard of her new home. Home — she had a house of her own to command.

ABOUT THE AUTHOR

Jennifer Mueller has travelled extensively because of her work as a Peace Corps volunteer. As a result, rafting on the Nile in Uganda, living in a Montana ghost town, African safaris, European youth hostels and the Black Hills of South Dakota all fill her scrapbooks. She has a background in forestry and enjoys studying history. Jennifer has one daughter and this is her first novel published by Robert Hale.

We hope you have enjoyed this Large Print book. Other Thorndike, Wheeler, Kennebec, and Chivers Press Large Print books are available at your library or directly from the publishers.

For information about current and upcoming titles, please call or write, without obligation, to:

Publisher
Thorndike Press
295 Kennedy Memorial Drive
Waterville, ME 04901
Tel. (800) 223-1244

or visit our Web site at:

http://gale.cengage.com/thorndike

OR

Chivers Large Print
published by BBC Audiobooks Ltd
St James House, The Square
Lower Bristol Road
Bath BA2 3SB
England
Tel. +44(0) 800 136919
email: bbcaudiobooks@bbc.co.uk
www.bbcaudiobooks.co.uk

All our Large Print titles are designed for easy reading, and all our books are made to last.